Marco & Rakia:

Not Your Ordinary Hood Kinda Love

Tina J

Copyright 2017

This novel is a work of fiction. Any resemblances to actual events, real people, living or dead, organizations, establishments or locales are products of the author's imagination. Other names, characters, places, and incidents are used fictionally.

Because of the dynamic nature of the Internet, any web address or links contained in this book may have changed since publication, and may no longer be valid.

More Books by Tina J

A Thin Line Between Me & My Thug 1-2
I Got Luv for My Shawty 1-2
Kharis and Caleb: A Different kind of Love 1-2
Loving You is a Battle 1-3
Violet and the Connect 1-3
You Complete Me
Love Will Lead You Back
This Thing Called Love
Are We in This Together 1-3
Shawty Down to Ride For a Boss 1-3
When a Boss Falls in Love 1-3
Let Me Be The One 1-2
We Got That Forever Love
Ain't No Savage Like The One I got 1-2
A Queen & Hustla 1-2 (collab)
Thirsty for a Bad Boy 1-2
Hasaan and Serena: An Unforgettable Love 1-2
We Both End Up With Scars
Are We in this Together 1-3
Caught up Luvin a beast 1-3
A Street King & his Shawty 1-2
I Fell for the Wrong Bad Boy 1-2 (collab)
Addicted to Loving a Boss 1-3
I need that Gangsta Love 1-2 (collab)
Still Luvin' a Beast 1-2
I Wanna Love You 1-2
When She's Bad, I'm Badder 1-3
Marco & Rakia 1-2

Rakia

"Catch the retard. Hurry up!" One of the boys yelled, after school.

"Fuck y'all." I stuck my finger up and kept walking.

"Yea, I bet you would like that." Another one shouted.

"Don't nobody want that special needs pussy." My mouth fell open. Did he really just say that? What is a special needs pussy anyway?

"Obviously, y'all do because you bother me everyday."

"What you say?" I took off running because the last thing I wanted to be, is raped. I've heard too many rape stories and I refused to be a statistic.

Oh, let me introduce myself. My name is Rakia Winters, I'm 18 years old and everyday, for the last four years; it has been pure hell in high school. Kids made fun of me because of my so-called disability, where I found myself, to be as normal as them. I guess because, I spoke a little slower than them and didn't indulge in pathetic, childish and stupid conversations, they assumed I had special needs. A person with anxiety issues, does not make you special.

Who wants to sit around all day listening to them speak about the girls they slept with, or listen to the petty ass girls, who talked about the number of dicks they sucked? I mean, if you ask me, they all too young to be having sex but if they're gonna do it, why discuss it? I wish, I would sleep with someone and tell. I learned a long time ago, never tell your friends or family who you like, or what you did. Most likely, they'll envy you and try to take the man. It's what my cousin Cara did to me. The guy, wasn't really my man but I staked claim on him first.

See, Cara lived down the street with her ghetto ass mother, Shanta; who happens to be my father's sister. She only lives this close because my aunt comes down here, every time my grandmother cooks and when they get paid. She may not be on drugs but she for sure, is a got damn beggar. And, I heard she be tricking but that's none of my business. I loved my aunt though because she had my back; a lot. Let me get back to my disgusting ass cousin.

5

There's this guy around the way, who I ran into last year by accident. I never knew his name and I wasn't aware of his status in the streets. He was big time though and I found that out the day we met, or should I say, he came around. To him, I probably looked like a weirdo but for me, it was love at first sight.

I was walking home from school and as usual, had to walk in front of the many guys, who posted and politicked in front of the bodega's. Most of them were playing dice, selling drugs or even standing there, doing absolutely nothing. I called them, LOSERS.

Anyway, a black truck pulled up with dark tinted windows and it looked like, it just came from the car wash. The driver stepped out, went to the back and opened the door. I saw this man's feet before him and I must say, a bitch was impressed. I may live a boring life but I follow a lot of celebrities on Instagram and know expensive shit, when I see it.

He was wearing a pair of Ferragamao shoes and I bet, the black dress socks were expensive too. He wore a suit, that

6

had gold cufflinks on the sleeves and a pair of black sunglasses.
I couldn't see his eyes and his body filled out the entire outfit. I
think he was some sort of Spanish decent because he had that
caramel complexion and long hair.

The people on the corner, literally started scrambling
to stand up and get it together. His presence screamed BOSS
and I was in love. He walked in the store and a few guys
followed, while the driver leaned against the car watching the
others. Now, I'm thinking they're cool, or something because
why would he not only, be leaning on the car but monitoring
what's going on out here.

It just so happened Cara and her messy ass friend
Angela, were with me. They were so engrossed in the niggas on
the side, they never paid attention to this beautiful specimen of
a man. See, whenever we walked this way, my cousin and
Angela, always had to add switch in their hips and flirt with
anyone who paid them any mind. Me; I'm usually rushing past
or leaving them but this day; I had to wait for him to come
back out. I had to see him, one more time. As I stood there,
Cara must've noticed and came over to me.

7

"*Ummm, you're usually rushing, or outta here by now. What's up?*" Before I could come up with an excuse, the fine man came back out.

"*DAMN! Who the hell is that?*" She yelled out, which made him look in our direction. I instantly put my head down.

"*Hey baby.*" She yelled and I wanted to smack her. He wasn't even my man and here I was, ready to throw hands with her. I can't fight for shit but I'd get my ass beat for him. That's how fine he was. He removed his shades and I fell in love even more, after meeting his gaze. Those eyes pierced straight through me and if I could jump in his car and go home with him, I would.

"*Shouldn't you be in school, or something?*" He asked and Cara became embarrassed.

"*I'm grown.*" She shouted and he looked her up and down before laughing.

"*A grown woman, wouldn't yell out at a man. She'd walk right up to him and present herself in a respectable manner.*"

"*WHAT?*" Now she was mad.

"That's what wrong with these young bitches now a days. Always screaming grown and act crazier and more childish, than a damn three-year-old."

"Fuck You!" All of a sudden, we heard a few guns cock. I turned my head and every last one of those men, had a gun pulled out on her. What the fuck type of control does this nigga, have on them? I stood there scared to death and so did Ang. What if they killed her? Cara had finally got herself in some shit.

"When you're in the presence of a BOSS, respect me. Or the next time, your two friends here; will be walking you home, without a fucking head. Don't fuck with me." He put his glasses back on and sat in the car.

"Oh, I'm gonna make sure to get that nigga in bed. You see that shit? I mean, I was scared for a minute but he definitely got me horny."

"Cara, I saw him first, you know that." Her and Angela looked at me and busted out laughing.

"Bitch, he don't want no fucking retard. What, you gonna do, invite him over to play blocks with you. Or maybe,

Tetris on your shitty phone, since that's your life besides

school. Girl, I'll find you someone, more of your speed." She

waved me off.

"NO CARA! I WANT HIM!"

"Are you really standing here pouting like a two-year-

old? This is exactly what he meant about not being grown.

Grow up and find your own man because he's mine." She

looped arms with Angela and they walked ahead of me,

discussing how she'd bed him. I was so angry, I went straight

home and cried.

I hadn't seen him since that day and good riddance.

Cara came by the house a few days later saying, she ran into

him again and they basically are a couple. I've never seen him

come around to pick her up or anything. When I ask, she says,

I'm either not home or asleep. From that day forward, I

learned my lesson and won't tell a soul about anyone, I found

attractive.

I never had anyone to teach me, to keep my mouth

closed when it came to men, because my parents were, or

should I say, are crackheads. I was born addicted to the drug they both loved. I was taken away from them, in the hospital of course and given to my grandparents on my father's side. They basically hated me, just as much and blamed me, for my mom getting him addicted. My mother's parents, wanted nothing to do with me because they knew, if I was in their care, my mom would always be there and they washed their hands of her. I don't blame either side, however; why would you hold a baby accountable for their mistakes?

Anyway, to my knowledge, I wasn't able to leave the hospital for a month, before I was placed with Addie and Earl. Two of the worst individuals, I ever met. When they did get me, I was told from my aunt Shanta, they only took me, to get a state check and food stamps. I don't know why they were receiving any assistance, when both of them worked but then again, my grandmother got paid under the table. Which means, they only went off my grandfather's income and he worked in a factory making a little above, minimum wage. My aunt didn't care for her parents either but she was cordial like I said, more or less for the free food and money they gave her.

Needless to say, my grandmother made a big meal every Sunday and cooked two small ones, two other days of the week. If I planned on eating during the week, I had to save whatever I had on my plate. There was no grabbing food out the pans, when I was done, to save. I had to literally pile food on my plate, just to put some away. *Ghetto, I know right.* My grandmother said, since I didn't pay any bills in the house, I only ate on the days she cooked. She had the nerve to say, if I had money, I'd be able to make my own meals. *Wait! Aren't the food stamps my money?* It no longer mattered because graduation is around the corner and I'm on the first thing smoking, out of here.

****

"How are you, Miss Winters?" My guidance counselor asked. We had two weeks left of school and I had all my credits, so I didn't have to take any exams, if I didn't want to.

"I'm good. Ready, to get outta this town. I wanna broaden my horizons and make something of myself. I also want to.-"

"Ok, Miss Winters, I get it." I put my head down.

12

"I'm sorry. You know, I tend to get carried away discussing my future. I mean, with the hand I was dealt, anyone would try and leave."

"I hear ya. If only we could all go."

"I'm sorry. I didn't mean to insinuate."

"No, its ok. I have to deal with it." I felt bad.

Mrs. Harris, lost her daughter two years ago, to a man she was married to. He claimed, he loved her to death and I guess he did because he sure killed her, for trying to leave him. After he killed her, he turned the gun on himself. Poor thing; even death couldn't keep him away from her. She wiped the few tears and looked at me. I loved Mrs. Harris and wished on many occasions that she was my mom. If only we had a choice, in the matter.

"So, I see you've been accepted to twenty different colleges." I smiled.

"Rakia, that's great but you only have two weeks left and you haven't decided where you're going to go."

"I know. I want to go to Harvard but I can't afford it." I was upset because even though Harvard is known for its outstanding law program, they also had an engineering program too.

"Honey, your grades and test scores are at a genius level. Harvard offered you a four-year scholarship, which means, everything is included and you won't have any student loans to pay back, once you graduate."

"Whhhattt. I mean what?" When I get excited or nervous, I ramble on and on but she stops me, every time. And when I get upset, I tend to stutter, mumble and pronounce things a little slower. This is why kids called me retarded.

"Yes. You will have everything you need. Look Rakia." She came from around her desk.

"Honey, this is a great opportunity and knowing your background, this is your chance to get out and find yourself. Don't let the name calling and mean things people said, get to you. Shit, half of them can't even graduate; including your cousin." She winked.

Cara was a year older and graduating with me, due to her getting left back last year. She never came to school and when she did, it was only for half the day. I tried to ask her what was wrong and she would claim, her man says, school takes up too much of her time. Little did she know; word on the street was, she became obsessed over some dude who didn't want her and spent her days trying to locate him.

"How fast can I leave, once I graduate?"

"Actually, there's a summer program for freshman that starts a week after you graduate. But you have to sign up for it before the end of today."

"Can we do it now?" I asked. I didn't have a computer at home and the phone I did have, is what they call the Obama phone. You know the one, the state gives you, if you're on assistance and you only get a certain number of minutes. My grandmother has an android and said she didn't want the piece of shit state phone and gave it to me. *Crazy, right?* I was only able to get on Instagram and send out college applications at the public library, or school but at least, I had something.

"Absolutely. And if you need anything, like luggage, clothes or money, let me know." I told her ok but knew damn well, I wasn't asking for any of it. All I wanted to do from this moment, is graduate and get the hell outta town and its exactly,

what I'm gonna do.

Cara

Today is finally my last day walking through the halls of this high school. I spent five years in this bitch and couldn't wait to get out. I should've graduated last year but following behind this stupid nigga, had me missing school days and basically failing. He didn't ask me to, but after being with him for two days, I figured we were a couple. No, he didn't say it and he only let me suck him off a few times, but still. You don't be around someone for two full days and not feel something for them. I mean, why the hell, would you even waste your time?

"You ready cuz?" Rakia asked, as she placed the hat on her head. I sucked my teeth at her.

I swear, the bitch got on my nerves. Not only was she like a fucking genius but her beauty captivates any nigga who comes around; which is why, I jumped on the BOSS nigga that day. I saw the way he removed his glasses and stared her down, when I yelled. I also knew, yelling would get his attention but he paid me no mind, until I tried him. He let my ass have it, in

17

a nice way and even though he embarrassed the hell out of me, I still wanted him.

"I'm ready to get away from your retarded ass."

"Why do you call me that?" She looked at me and I hated how innocent she really was. Rakia, has never done anything to me and was always trying to be my friend, even though we're blood related but I hated her.

"Because it's what you are.

"But I'm not Cara. I may stutter a little and ramble on a lot but you of all people know

how smart I am." I sucked my teeth.

She's right though. Me and everyone else, knew exactly, how much of a genius she is. Hell, she's the valedictorian and the only one in the school, who was accepted to a shitload of colleges. All she does is, go to school, the library and go home, right after. Her life is boring, which is another reason, why I couldn't understand why men wanted her.

She rolled her eyes and continued to fix her cap. I wasn't jealous of my cousin because she was pretty. Hell, I was just as gorgeous, standing at five foot six, with a light skinned complexion, a bad ass body and my weave, hair and nails, stayed done, complimentary of my mom's tricks. I didn't like her because she was smarter than me. I know it sounds crazy but being a beautiful and smart black woman, will get the attention of any man; legal or not. I knew, if she found a man, he'll wife her up quick and I couldn't have that. I'm the oldest and should be the first at everything.

"Well, you don't have to wait any longer. Its time." She walked out and if I could donkey kick her in the back, I would, just because.

After the graduation, Mrs. Harris came up to Rakia, while we were talking to my grandmother and other family members, and asked her to come in the parking lot. All of us followed and to say a bitch was in her feelings from what I saw, would be putting it mildly. There was a big ass red bow on the top of a brand new, Champagne colored, Mercedes truck. The temp tags were on it and you could tell it's never been driven.

"Do you like it?" Rakia asked if it were hers and once she said yes, she started crying.

"Mrs. Harris, I can't accept this."

19

"You can, and you will." She handed her the keys and Rakia unlocked the door. I'm not gonna front, a bitch opened the passenger side door and hopped in. The seats were cream and the steering wheel, had a Champagne trim around it. There was Bluetooth, a BOSE radio, navigation, back up cameras and a bunch of other shit, I kept pressing the buttons to.

"Hmph. Where did you get this type of money from and why you buy this for my granddaughter?" If anyone knew Mrs. Harris, they knew she didn't take kind to disrespect. I tried to get out fast and stop her but it was too late.

"First of all… Rakia is a grown woman, regardless of you, continuously treating her like a child and stealing her state checks." My grandmother looked straight at Rakia, who shrugged her shoulders. I knew she didn't tell because she never wanted anyone to place her in foster care, if they found out my grandmother wasn't providing for her. Rakia, rather live with my grandparents, then move place to place.

Second… I didn't buy this for her. The college she's attending, heard about her financial situation and being she's going to their school, they purchased this for her."

"Why would they do that? She's not an athlete." I asked, assuming only coaches did that, when they were trying to bribe them to attend their school for sports.

"No, but they love her mind. I'm not sure if you know or care but Rakia is a genius. She aced every test she's ever taken in school and had a perfect score on the IQ test, which only 1% of Americans, can do. This car is only minor, compared to what they have to offer. You see Cara, while you and the rest of the kids in school called her retarded, stupid, and the other names to hurt her, she used her brain to beat y'all. What I mean by that is, she's going places in life."

"What's that supposed to mean?" My grandmother asked.

"It means, she won't need y'all for shit and don't call her, when you're doing bad. Don't try and distract her and last but not least, if any of you, even think about trying to get her kicked out of school, let's just say, I won't have a problem coming to her aide." She smirked and walked over to me.

"You're right about the school only purchasing things for students, if they're an athlete." She whispered in my ear and I looked at her. My grandmother and everyone else were drooling over Rakia's truck.

"I brought this with my hard-own money because she deserves it, after all your jealous ass put her through and if you tell her, I'll make you regret it." She patted my shoulder and walked off.

"Rakia, I'm proud of you." My mom said and gave her a hug. They've always been tighter than, she and I. It's like my mom felt bad for Rakia's parents being crackheads. That's fine but she did have a daughter too.

"Thanks aunt Shanta. You wanna go for a ride?"

"Maybe tomorrow. I want you to go out and celebrate graduating and going to a prestigious school."

"I don't have anywhere to go." She put her head down.

"You can go with me and Angela, to the club. Cardi B and Migos will be there."

"REALLY!" She got all excited. I only invited her, so we could show off in her truck. Call me what you want but a bitch was showing up in style.

"Yup. Be ready by eleven."

"Thanks so much, Cara. Wait! I don't have anything to wear."

"Here's some money girls. Go to the mall and ball out." My mom handed me a knot of money and snatched it back before I could see how much it was. She peeled off six hundred dollars and handed it to Rakia. She said it was her graduation present from her. I knew it was from one of her many men, but fuck it. We about to ball out.

****

"I'm not sure about this outfit Cara. I mean, it's really short and I've never wore a pair of heels." Rakia complained and Angela sucked her teeth. We were at my house getting ready for the club and here she was nervous, to put on the outfit, she picked out.

It was a short black strapless dress. It came down to her knees and she purchased some nice ass, Steve Madden heels. I flat ironed her hair, that came down her back and Angela did her make up. My cousin was always pretty but tonight, she looked like an entirely different person.

"You look very pretty Rakia. Live free for once."
Angela told her but you could still see how uncomfortable she
was.

"I wish my brother was in better health, to see how
beautiful you are." My mom said and came in to take some
photos of us.

"Me too, aunt Shanta. I tried asking him and my mom,
to get better but they wave me off and ask me to leave them
alone."

"I know baby. They're both really sick and I promise
you, if they ever come to me for help, I'll be the first one to
offer my services."

"Thank you." She hugged my mom tight. Angela
looked at me and I shrugged my shoulders. She knows my
mom is devastated over her brother being on drugs and to see
his daughter, turn out the way she did, regardless of how my
grandparents treated her, made my mom's day.

"Ok, let's be out. Bye mom."

"Be careful and Cara." She pulled me back.

"Yea."

"I know you can't stand Rakia and only using her for her truck but listen to me and listen to me well." I tried to snatch away from my mom but she wasn't having it.

"She is very naive to these streets, Cara."

"I know ma."

"You better fucking watch her. If anything and I mean anything, happens to her, you'll have me to deal with. Do I make myself clear?"

"Yes." I may have a smart-ass mouth and nasty attitude but the one person I didn't fuck with, is my mom. She is one gangsta ass bitch and honestly, I ain't ready for those hands. I tried my luck once and she beat my ass, like a stranger off the street.

I walked off the porch and to the truck, where Angela and Rakia, were in a deep discussion about building some machine to help cancer patients. My cousin, kept her head in the books and when I tried to have conversations with her; half the time, she'd go into discussing other shit, like this. I had to take a double look at Angela though, who seemed to be intrigued by what they were speaking about. Angela isn't dumb; however, I didn't know she knew anything about engineering either.

****

"Oh my God, Cara. Look at the line. How are we going to get in there?" Rakia asked and slowly drove in the valet line.

"I got this." I pulled my cell out and dialed up Trey. He's a bouncer at the club and always let me skip the line. Of course, I had to return the favor eventually. I didn't mind though, because what he was working with, is definitely a reason to keep going back.

"Ok. Hand the guy your keys and Trey, is at the door waiting for us." At first, she was nervous but once the guy helped her out the car and said how pretty she was, all that went out the window.

We stepped in the club and it was already half way full. Trey led us over to a table, close to the VIP section, which only held ballers. I say that because those sections cost over five thousand to have, when events like this went down. Plus, they get strippers and a few bottles of Ace of Spades, courtesy of the owner. I guess, if you spend that kind of money in here, the

26

owner had to thank you somehow. The waitress came over and took our orders. The good thing about this club, was if you looked mature, they didn't card you. After about two Martinis and a few shots, all of us were feeling tipsy.

"This is my song." Rakia yelled out and went on the dance floor.

I ain't no stuck-up chick, I ain't picky, I just want, what's best for me, I can't let nobody get the best of me, part time love ain't my destiny, I ain't no stuck-up chick, I ain't picky, I just want, what's best for me, I can't let nobody get the best of me, unless they want the best for me.

The song Easy, by Demetria McKinney played and my cousin did her thing. I had no idea, she could move the way, she was. When I say, she had the attention of almost every man in there, I meant it. I even saw the ballers in the VIP area, stand up to watch her. One person, in particular stood out and it seemed like, he was in a zone watching her. The way he put the cup to his lips and sipped, without taking his eyes off her, pissed me off, even more. He never stared at me like that.

"Ok, everyone. It's time. Make some noise for the Number 1, artist in the country right now. Miss Cardi B." The DJ announced and Rakia, made her way back to the table. Cardi, started to perform Bodak Yellow and the crowd went nuts. My attitude went from zero to hundred real quick, when I noticed the guy from VIP, still had his eyes on my cousin.

"I'm ready to go." I said and both her and Angela, looked at me. It's obvious they were enjoying themselves.

"But she just came out. I'm not ready." Rakia whined, only pissing me off more.

"I said let's go. My mom, said I had to watch you, so you have to leave, when I do." She pouted and started grabbing her things. We all stood up and was about to walk, until four dudes stood in front of us.

"Excuse us." One of the guys made a way for me to leave and moved right back, to block Rakia in."

"Ummm. We're together so, if you'll kindly excuse me." I hated she was such a geek and spoke proper.

"I'm sorry miss but I can't let you leave." The guy's voice was aggressive and scary.

"Cara, what's going on?" She looked around the guys at me and I didn't know what to do.

"Boss, wants to see you."

"Boss? Who is Boss and why does he have you blocking me in?" He pointed up to the VIP section and there he was again, this time staring down at us. Rakia, never looked and continued to converse with the guards.

"Tell your Boss, I've been here for a few hours now and if he wanted to converse with me, he should have done so, sooner. As you can see, my cousin is ready to call it a night. If you'll excuse me."

"Rakia, come on." I tried getting in between the guys.

"You can walk up the steps willingly, or I'll carry you. It's your choice." One of the guys said.

"Are you serious? I don't want to meet your boss. I have to go."

"Fine." He reached out for her and she smacked his hand away.

"I'll walk. Come on Cara and Angela." She said and we went behind her. When we reached the section, some guy was blocking us from going further.

"Nah, only shorty right here can come in." He grabbed Rakia's hand.

"Please don't leave me. I'll be right back." I could see how nervous my cousin was but it didn't stop her from going in.

"Fuck this. I'm leaving." I turned around and Angela stood there with her arms folded.

"You can't leave her Cara."

"Why not? She left us, to go with him."

"If something happens to her, your mom will kill you."

"I'm just gonna tell her, she refused to leave with me, now come on."

"I'm gonna wait right here."

"WHAT? You don't even like her."

"Cara, it doesn't matter if I do or not. We came together, we leave together."

"Ok, what about me?"

"You're choosing to leave because the nigga chose her but you need to wait too."

"I'm good. I hope both of y'all get raped together." I left her standing there with her mouth hanging open. She knew not to try me.

I called an Uber and waited outside for it. If my mom asks, I'll tell her exactly what happened. Rakia, was being grown and left with some nigga, no matter how much, I begged her not to. Shit, its half true anyway.

Rakia

I was having the time of my life, when outta nowhere, Cara caught an attitude and was ready to go. I don't even know why she behaved that way, when she invited me here. Her attitude only aggravated me and I didn't want her to cause a scene.

And let's not mention the huge guys who stopped us from leaving, scared me to death. Once they let me know, I only had two choices and that's walk or be carried, I chose to walk. I didn't know them, nor where their hands been. No man will touch my body, unless I want him too; no exceptions.

Anyway, after reaching the top of the stairs, some guy looked at Cara and then back at me, before saying she couldn't enter. It was an uncomfortable situation and all I wanted to do, was see who this guy was and leave. I walked behind him and unfortunately, the VIP section was so crowded and full of weed smoke, I found myself fanning my way through, to reach this person. However, once I did, my heart skipped a beat.

There he sat. The man, of my dreams. The one Cara staked claim on, over a year ago, even after, I asked her not to. The one, I wanted badly, sat in front of me looking like an expensive piece of art. His hair was brushed back in a ponytail. The jeans and fitted shirt, showed more of his muscles off and tattoos, I didn't see before. I mean, his body was covered. And those eyes pierced through my soul, once again. I wanted to say hello but the words wouldn't come out.

"It's pretty crowded in here. You wanna go somewhere else to talk?" He smiled and stood up.

"Ummm. Surrrreee." I could kill myself for getting so excited and stuttering. It didn't seem to bother him though. His hand intertwined with mine and he led me to another room, behind the wall. What the hell type of shit, this club got going on?

We walked up another flight of steps and into a different room. It was very nice and had a few couches in it, a TV, mini bar and you could see the club from the glass. I walked over to it and noticed Angela sitting at the bar but couldn't spot Cara. I sent Angela a text and said, I'd be down

33

shortly and begged her not to leave me. I got her number at the mall earlier because her and Cara wanted to go in other stores. Cara didn't have her phone and the only way to find them, was to get Angela's. At this moment, I'm glad, I did. She had the phone in her hand and could tell when it went off. Once she text back she wouldn't, it put me at ease.

"You ok?" I smelled his cologne when he stood behind me.

"Ummm. Yea." I moved from in front of him. I didn't want him getting any ideas.

"Am I making you nervous?"

"To be honest, I've never been this close to any man, besides my cousin, my father and grandfather. I mean, there are the stupid boys in school but they're not men. Or you can count the guys at the grocery store but then again, they don't speak to me." He moved closer to me.

"You ramble, when you're nervous, I see." He pushed my hair on the side of my ear and lifted my chin to look at him.

"Damn, you're beautiful." My face felt like it turned beet red.

"Thank you." I cleared my throat and moved away.

"You speak proper too." I know he didn't ask to speak with me, to hear how I talk.

"Why did you want to converse with me?"

"I see you're out here on your grown woman shit." I gave him a crazy look.

"Ok, I guess."

"What I mean by that is, the dress is short but not too short. The dance you did was sensual and erotic, instead of twerking and showing off your assets. And you captivated just about every man in here tonight. Who are you and what's your story?" Each time he stared at me, I felt like he could read every thought in my mind.

"It's pretty long and I don't have time to speak on it. My friend Angela is downstairs waiting on me. See, I'm the designated driver and.-" His lips crashed on mine and I almost jumped in his arms. This was my first kiss, so hopefully, I was doing it right. He pushed me against the glass and pressed his pelvis on mine. I swear, if I even thought, I'd know how to handle a man like him, I'd forget all my morals and be a hoe.

35

"Mmmmm. We have to stop."

"My bad ma."

"But, you taste so good." I grabbed the back of his neck and pulled him in for another kiss.

"Stay with me tonight." He asked, when he pulled back.

"WHAT? I don't know what type of chick you think I am but you got the wrong one buddy." I started grabbing my things and he threw them out my hand.

"I could sleep with any bitch in here tonight but I don't want none of them." I sucked my teeth at his arrogant statement.

"I asked you to stay with me, so I could learn more about you. What's your likes and dislikes? What makes you laugh and what makes you cry? What do you wanna be in life? Things like that. You intrigue the hell outta me and if you leave, I'm not sure you'll come back." I stared at him.

"Why wouldn't I come back?"

"You don't know?"

"Know what?"

"Nothing. Let me walk you out."

36

"But, I thought you just asked me to stay the night with you." Don't ask me why, I even said that.

"Are you tryna fuck?" How did he go from, not fucking to wanting to? He was confusing the hell out of me.

"I don't know the first thing about you and you're trying to get me to open my legs. I think not mister, whoever you are." I picked my things up and headed to the door.

"You're right about one thing though. After I leave, you definitely won't see me again. Goodbye." I opened the door and slammed it behind me. I had no idea where I was going and the guard must've known because he pointed in an opposite direction.

"Let's go." I said to Angela, who was drinking at the bar and talking to some guy.

"Are you ok?"

"Yes. If you're not ready, I'll wait for you in the truck." I looked up and the guy was staring down at me, from the VIP section. When did he leave the room?

"No, I'm good. Thanks for keeping me company." She said to the guy. I looked up one last time before leaving and the so-called man of my dreams, had some chick dancing in front of him. She was barley dressed and even though, he wasn't my man, it pissed me off. I don't need anyone in my life like him anyway.

****

"Rakia, I just want to say from the bottom of my heart, I really am sorry for the way I've treated you all these years." I pulled over and looked at her.

"Angela, are you ok?"

"Yes."

"Where did all this come from?"

"Tonight, we were having a good time and all of a sudden, your petty ass cousin got in her feelings about the dude wanting you and not her. I told her, I wasn't leaving you here and she said, she hoped we both got raped."

"WHAT?"

"I know." She shook her head.

"Cara, has a mean streak to her and its worse then you've ever seen. Be lucky, you didn't spend a lot of time with her."

"But why is she mad at me? Cara told me last year, her and the guy had a fling but they didn't last long. I may not be in the streets but I do know, they were never together the way she says. He dissed her every time he ran into her and evidently, she's been with someone else. Now, if she had messed with him, I would've never entertained him. I've never been with a guy but I damn sure wouldn't be with one, she had."

"Rakia. Honestly, I don't know if she ever did mess with him. She always told me the same and I heard, what you heard. I do know, she probably said it so you wouldn't mess with him. But forget about them. I want us to be friends."

"Huh?"

"Look. I know you're going away to school and contrary to what Cara may have told you, I am very smart and actually going to NYU in the fall. I also applied for the summer program, just to get away from here."

"Angela, that's great and I truly appreciate the apology. I've gone through my juvenile years alone and with no friends. If you're truly serious about being my friend, with no hidden agendas, then I'm all for it. But if you lie or hurt me, I won't ever speak to you again."

"One thing, I don't do, is lie. I'm telling you now, I keep it a hundred at all times, even if it means telling you things you may not want to hear."

"That's what friends do, right?"

"Yup." I went back to driving.

"Hey, why don't you stay over my house and we can go out to breakfast in the morning."

"Ummm."

"Its ok Rakia. I know, you're not used to people being nice to you but I'm being serious. I just want to make up for the hurtful things, I may have said or done over the years."

"Fine. Let me run home and grab an outfit."

"Ok. And Rakia."

"Yea."

"Stop letting Cara get to you. I know people say mean things to you but she's your cousin. She's supposed to have your back before anyone."

"I always ask myself, why she's so mean to me and to this day, I still don't know why."

"Its because you're better than her."

"But, I'm not."

"Oh, but you are. Let's get to my house and I'll fill you in on why you are."

****

"Are you sure, we can go?" I asked Angela on our way to some block party. The night I slept over, she told me everything Cara and her, used to say about me. I respected her more because most people don't tell you their part.

"Yes. I told you the guy from the club wants us to come."

"Us."

"He said, you and your friends. He knew, I wouldn't come alone. Unfortunately, I did invite Cara, just because I'm sure she'd see photos on Instagram or something."

"Fine! Do I look ok?" I checked myself over in the mirror. I had on a pair of denim shorts, that didn't have my ass hanging out, a spaghetti strap shirt and a pair of strap up, flip flops. I wasn't trying to catch a man, when I'm leaving tomorrow for school.

"You look fine girl. Now come on so we can pick your petty ass cousin up." I grabbed her arm.

"Angela, I don't want her to know, I slept over, or that we've discussed the other issues."

"Why not? Rakia, I'm trying to be better and you're making it hard." She started laughing.

"Its not that Angela. I feel like we became very close over the last week and I don't want her destroying everything, with her mouth. I'm sure you told me everything you said but I don't need her reminding me because she's upset." We got in the truck and she agreed.

"Why are you in the back?"

"Because she'll know something, if I sit in the front. Its bad enough, we have to tell her, you saw me at the store." Angela rolled her eyes. I understood where she was coming from but I also didn't want any problems with Cara. She has the tendency to embarrass the hell out of me, in public.

42

We pulled up in front of my aunt's house and Cara may as well, have come out naked. Her ass and chest were hanging out. The shoes were cute but she caught an attitude, the minute she hopped in the truck.

"It's about time. I only been waiting since yesterday to get there." I didn't say anything.

"Be happy, I invited your ass, after what the fuck you said about being raped." Cara waved her off. Angela moved up and put her head in between the console.

"If you ever wish some shit like that on me again, I'll whoop your ass." I looked in my rearview mirror. Angela had a look on her face, that told me, she isn't to be fucked with.

"Now let's go have a good time." She said it so calm and then sat back in her seat. I thought, Cara would respond but she didn't. All this time, I assumed Angela was scared of Cara, but right now, shit looks funny.

"Damn! Look at all these fine niggas." Cara yelled out and since the window was down, some looked in our direction. She always spoke of her mom being ghetto, yet, she's the same.

Angela pulled her phone out and called up the guy, who invited us. I heard, her asking where he was and she pointed over to a group of guys. Cara adjusted her shirt to show more cleavage, as if she needed to and we made our way over to them. It didn't take long for the guy she spoke to, to come over. And damn, he was fucking gorgeous too. I mean shit, they really do travel in packs. I gave her a thumbs up and found a chair to sit in. I knew, she had been talking and texting this dude all week but this is my first time seeing him up close. I didn't really pay him any mind at the club but she definitely got a winner. I hope he doesn't cheat. Men that fine, usually had tons of women on the side.

"I'll be back Rakia." Cara walked away and left me alone. I'm used to it though.

I stood and went over to grab a burger and a soda, only to be snatched away. I didn't even get upset because he wore the same cologne, the night we met. I sure hope, my inner hoe doesn't come out today. Fuck it! If it does; I'm gone in the morning anyway.

Marco

I spotted her, the second she stepped out the truck and I must say, a nigga was impressed. She looked beautiful without showing as much as, these other bitches. Tech, told me this chick he met, was coming with friends but who knew, she was the one from the night, at the club? I wasn't expecting her but she damn sure won't be outta my sight, now that she is. That's why, when she made her way to grab something to eat, I snatched her right up. I don't need none of these thirsty ass niggas trying to press up on my future. I'm not gonna say wife because a nigga ain't settling down like that. I'm young and a chick has to string me the fuck out, to get on one knee. Shit, I been with Bobbi, for over three years and I damn sure ain't marrying her. Hell, I won't even give her my seeds.

If you don't already know, my name is Marco Santiago. I'm 26, mixed with black and Spanish and I'm the motherfucking plug, to these fake ass dope boys. Don't get me wrong, I'm cool with them but like most niggas hustling; they lazy as hell. They wanna get on the corner, whenever they feel like it and half the time, can't even afford the weight, they ask for. How the hell you tryna come up and can't even make the money you need to re-up? I'm not a credit nigga either. If you don't have the money, it's obvious you won't get the product.

Yes, I have law enforcement on my payroll, as most connects and plugs do. Sad to say, but you won't get far without them. Who cares, if they get a small portion of the money, I make. It's nothing compared to what I'm bringing in. If you wanna know; a nigga makes close to a million dollars, every other week. And before you start saying it's unrealistic, never think of it like that; especially, when a nigga, has quite a few states under his belt. You don't get rich or should I say wealthy, by supplying one area.

Anyway, Bobbi and I, met at the strip club and yes, she was a stripper. Her body was and still is bad. However, she doesn't do it for me, other than sexually. She's a freak and will let me do whatever, I want. Unfortunately, I need a smart woman. Someone who can stimulate my mind and make me think about shit. Someone who doesn't spend all day in the house and all night out, doing whatever. Yea, I keep tabs on her but it didn't stop her from fucking other dudes. You may wonder, why I'm still with her, if I know for a fact she's with niggas. That's easy. The bitch is a certified freak and she'll do whatever, with no questions asked.

I won't fill her in on any of my business aspects but if I want a threesome, foursome or a damn orgy, guess who's down. If I want, her to get up at four in the morning to make me breakfast, or even go out and get it, guess who does it? If I want, my floors cleaned with a toothbrush, guess who'll do it. Exactly! So, you get where I'm going with it. I need a woman who's gonna tell me, HELL NO, or nigga, I wish you would cheat on me. Someone who isn't worried about the amount of money she can spend and in the process, let me do what I want. Bobbi, is the type of chick, to let anything fly, just so bitches can think she's the main chick. Little does she know, the position is about to be filled, shortly.

"This is the second time you bullied your way into my life." She said. I don't even recall getting shorty's name.

"What's your name ma?" I asked and pulled her in between my legs, as I leaned on my truck.

"Really! You don't know my name?" I shrugged my shoulders.

"You never told me and before you ask, I'm Marco."

"Well, nice to meet you Marco. I'm Rakia and do they have to go everywhere you do?" She pointed to the four guards standing around the truck.

"It's a lot you don't know about me shorty but if you must know; yes, they do." I put my face in her neck, when she took a bite of her burger. Whatever smell she had on, almost had me take her in the back seat. She smelled so good, I was semi hard. I guess she felt it too because she backed up and shook her head.

"What?" I adjusted myself.

"That?" She used her eyes to look at my dick.

"Shit, you turn me on. And then you smell good and your skin is soft."

"I'm sure you've met other women, who have the same affect." I pulled her back to me.

"Yea. But they're not you."

"Smooth." She smiled and I had to put my head down. Shorty, was doing something to me.

"You like that, huh?" She ate the last piece of her burger and sipped on her soda. She was even sexy doing that. I could see her getting me in a world of trouble.

We stood there talking and laughing for a while. She was definitely a breath of fresh air. I could tell when I said something to make her nervous, she'd ramble on about absolutely nothing. When she got excited about what she wanted to be in the future, she'd stutter a little. I could also tell she was a virgin and if she wasn't, whoever hit it first, had no clue what he was doing. No, I didn't touch her inappropriately I could tell by how nervous she got, each time she felt my dick on her ass, if I hugged her from behind. Shorty, had so much innocence behind her; I was definitely gonna have fun with her.

Out the corner of my eye, I could see Cara staring hard as hell. She knew not to say shit to me and she would never make it past my guards anyway. Cara, is a mistake that should've never happened. I swear, if I could erase that part of my life, I would.

The day she tried calling me out at the bodega, I had my eyes on Rakia. She was fucking beautiful to me and I wanted her. She had a medium brown complexion, her hair was long; and not to mention, she had a baby face. Her body was banging and even then; I knew she'd be perfect for me. Unfortunately, I had to embarrass the shit outta Cara and didn't give a fuck.

Two days later, I ran into Cara again at the same bodega and she cornered me in the store. The bitch was talking about doing all this freaky shit to me. I let her go on and after a few minutes of listening to the shit, I asked her age. Once she told me she was 19, I said fuck it and had her get in the car. I had to drive to New York for a meeting and took her with me. The way I saw it was, I could get my dick wet and still handle business. *Why did, I do that?* It was the worst two days, I ever had in my life. All she did was nag and complain about wanting me to fuck her, but once I fingered her, she acted like it was too much so I only let her suck my dick.

50

The first time, the bitch gagged so much, she threw up on the floor. I got up, took a shower and left. That night, I let her do it again and she did a better job. I guess she watched some movies or something, while I was gone. Sad to say, I allowed her to do it again, in the morning and on the drive back to Jersey, just to keep her from talking. I dropped her off and blocked her ASAP. The bitch started calling me from other numbers, showing up at places I was and a few times, I caught her stalking me at restaurants. The bitch was crazy. Now she got her face turned up because, her friend has my attention and not on no sexual type shit. I'm sure she can't comprehend, why I want her but it's not for anyone to know.

"MARCO!" I snapped my neck and saw Bobbi walking over with her hood rat ass friends.

"Let me get your number so I can handle this shit, right quick." I was hoping she didn't let Bobbi, keep her from doing so. She started reading off the number and stopped at the last four digits. My head was down so I didn't know why, until I looked up.

"Hmph. She's cute. How long you gonna be fucking this one?"

"Excuse me!" Rakia had her arms folded.

"You heard me. You're a cute one, which means, he'll most likely fuck you a few times and throw you away."

"Ummm. We're friends." Rakia looked at me nervously.

"Friends. Well, let me tell you this." Already knowing Rakia, is somewhat scary, I had to intervene.

"Aye, shut the fuck up Bobbi." I looked at one of the guards and he snatched her up but not without her screaming all types of shit to Rakia, about fucking her up, next time she sees her.

"Rakia." I grabbed her arm and she snatched away.

"I don't know why, I thought you'd be available."

"What's that supposed to mean?"

"It means, I've had a crush on you, since I first saw you at the bodega. Then you supposedly mess with Cara, and I won't say you did because she's known to make shit up. But then, you pursue me at the club and here, only for me to find out you're not only taken, but dealing with someone who wants to fight me on sight. Marco, I'm not for the bullshit and had I known this would happen. I would've walked away."

"Let me take you out and explain everything."

"No thanks. I don't need your stalkers coming for me."

"What?" She pointed to Cara who still had a snarl on her face and then at Bobbi, who was standing by my truck, fuming.

"I'm tryna get to know you. Fuck them."

"I'm sorry. I can't have fighting and getting arrested on my record. I'm trying to make something of myself and get out of here. I can see, she's gonna be a problem so instead of risking my future for a man, with his own issues. I'll walk away now before you insert pain in my life. It was nice meeting you."

DAMN! Is all I could say, as she walked away. I respected her decision because I knew she wanted a better life. I walked back over to my truck and snatched Bobbi up by her long ass weave. That was another thing about Rakia. I could tell all her hair was real.

"What the fuck is wrong with you?" I tossed her against the tree and watched her body bounce off. No, I'm not a woman beater but I'll fuck a bitch up, if need be.

"Marco, how you gonna disrespect me out in the open?" I laughed and lit a black and mild.

"Bitch are you crazy? We ain't no fucking couple. You may have some wife privileges but that's all they are."

"Marco, really?"

"Do you have a key to my house, or any of my whips?" She put her head down.

"I can't hear you."

"No."

"Do you have access to my money? Do I take you shopping? Do I pay any of your bills?"

"No."

"EXACTLY! So don't come over here tryna come for a woman, I'm speaking to because you think she's gonna take your spot."

"Well, is she?" She folded her arms.

"She would've, if you didn't fuck shit up." I moved over to my truck and leaned on it.

"What you doing, yo?"

"I'm apologizing." She unbuckled my jeans and started giving me head, in the parking lot. I told you, she'll do anything. I looked around to make sure no one was coming and let my head rest on the truck. I opened my eyes after she let me bust down her throat and was stuck.

FUCK!

Cara

Was I in my feelings, seeing how attentive Marco was being to my cousin? Absolutely! He never took the time out to converse with me, nor did he show me off in front of everyone, like he did her. We may be at a block party but I caught all the niggas smirking, as they looked at him. I even heard one say, they hope this chick is the one because he needs someone to calm him down. I swore, I told her ass he was mine and now she sninning and grinning in his face. He didn't make it any better, by feeling all over her and kissing on her neck and shit. At least, it didn't last long because after crazy ass Bobbi, went over there, Rakia walked away. Yea, I knew who she was. Hell, everyone knew her because she made sure to shut any bitch down, talking to Marco. Word on the street is, she's obsessed over him.

My cousin doesn't like drama at all; especially, when it comes to a guy. It's the exact reason she didn't fight with me, when I told her Marco, was mine. She sucked her teeth, pouted and probably cried, when she got home. She is a big ass cry baby, too. Anytime, someone hurts her feelings, she'll walk away, go hide and let the tears fall. Me, on the other hand, will run my mouth and get into an altercation or two, if a bitch came at me sideways. Yea, I let Angela get that off in the truck because I was dead wrong for wishing rape on them. However, she better not come for me again. I peeped her and Rakia, pretending to be best friends all of a sudden. Little did she know, the guy she likes Tech, ain't shit either. I'll expose him too, if need be.

"Are you ready to go?" Rakia asked and honestly, I was. No niggas were really talking to me and now that I see, how hurt she was, I'm in my glory.

"Yea, let's see if Angela is ready." I switched my ass over to where she was, with Tech. Now, he was as fine as, Marco. A nigga nonetheless but fine as hell.

"We ready to go."

"Bitch, beat it." Tech said and all he did was piss me off.

"What, nigga?"

"You heard me." He stood up and towered over me.

"She came with Rakia and when she's ready, then she'll go. Until then, get your ho ass, the fuck away from this table." I glanced around and noticed everyone looking; including Rakia and Angela.

"Oh, you trying to be funny. Nigga, I'll tell her everything." He chuckled.

"And I'll kill you where you stand. Don't fuck with me, Cara. I'm not those other niggas out here."

"Its ok Tech. Baby, Rakia is ready to go. I'll call you later." He turned around and stared at her.

"I'm not ready for you to go. Come on, why don't you stay a little longer?"

"You know, I don't leave my friends." She gave me a dirty look.

"I know, but.-"

"Call me when you finish here and maybe, I'll let you scoop me up."

"Maybe, my ass. I'll be over shortly. I only have you for one more day. I'm not tryna, let you outta my sight, until it's time for you to leave." What the hell did these bitches do, to get these niggas to fall, or even, showcase them? He kissed her softly on the lips, gave Rakia a hug and me the evilest glare, I've ever seen. Between him and Marco, I don't know who's the worst.

"Well, I guess its goodbye ladies." Rakia said, as we walked towards the truck.

"I'm leaving out, in exactly seven hours, so I won't. Hold on." She stopped herself and walked over to where Marco's truck was. We weren't parked that far away, so it didn't take long to witness what she did. Bobbi, looked like she had just finished sucking the skin off his dick. He was so engrossed in releasing, he didn't realize we could see.

"FUCK!" You heard him shout when he opened his eyes.

"I thought about asking Tech for your number, so I could call you but never mind." She said and turned to walk away.

"Rakia, hold on." He had the nerve to run over to her, pulling up his jeans. If I were Bobbi, I'd feel some kind of way.

She just sucked him off and he running to another bitch. She hit the alarm on the truck and sat down. He caught the door before she closed it.

"Look ma."

"Don't." She put her hand up. He smacked it down and I could see the anger building on his face.

"For future references shorty, don't ever put your hands in my face, or on me. I don't take kindly to disrespect."

"I'm sorry. I didn't mean to disrespect you. I wouldn't want you to do it to me; well, you did but whatever."

"I didn't do anything to you. Shorty, you're not my girl. I can do what I want. Maybe here isn't the place to get my dick sucked but who the fuck cares?"

"I did, actually."

"Why?"

"Marco, even though she made me angry, I still enjoyed talking to you. We could've been friends but this is too much. I mean, who lets a woman suck his dick in the parking lot? If I had a man, he would never have me doing anything to degrade myself in front of hundreds of people. Anyone could've walked up." He shrugged his shoulders.

"Look shorty. Maybe you were right."

"About?"

"I'm not a passive type of nigga and have the ability to fuck your whole life up, so let's just let shit go. Maybe, we'll see each other around."

"Lucky for you, I leave tomorrow, so this face won't ever grace your presence again." She started the car and he slammed her door. He was really mad.

"Get the fuck on yo, before I really get pissed." His chest was moving faster. Was he feeling Rakia that hard?

"Marco, you just said.-" She tried to speak.

"GO!" Rakia jumped when he yelled. Shit, we all did.

"Just pull off Rakia. He's capable of doing a lot more than yelling and you don't wanna be on the opposite end of it." Angela was getting on my nerves. I wanted to know why she even said a word. I would've loved to see him hook off on her, or something.

****

61

"Open the door Angela." I had to grab some of my things from her house, before she left for school. Rakia, ended up leaving way before her time and I gave zero fucks. Maybe, she'll crash on the way up the but I can't be so lucky.

"WHAT THE FUCK YOU BANGING ON HER DOOR FOR? ITS SEVEN IN THE DAMN MORNING." Tech shouted when he opened it. What the hell was he doing here? Then I remembered, Angela's parents went on a cruise a few days ago, for their wedding anniversary.

"I need to get my stuff before she leaves." He slammed the door in my face. I was about to go, when Angela came to the door. All she had on was a short ass robe.

"Damn, you wasted no time fucking him."

"Cara, for your information, we didn't have sex. I may be standing here in a robe and yes he slept over but not everyone has to fuck a man, in order to keep his attention." I sucked my teeth.

"Can I get my flatiron and shoes?"

"You couldn't wait?"

"Angela, you're leaving in a few hours."

"Ok. You could've come then. Look Cara." She closed the door and stepped on the porch.

"I'm not sure why you and Tech don't get along and really, I don't care. What I don't like, is you showing up this early in the morning for some shit, you could've waited on."

"Are you gonna give me my shit, or not?" The door opened.

"Where her shit at yo?"

"In my bedroom, hanging on the closet door." He walked away, came back and tossed my shit on the ground. I heard my flatiron crack.

"Nigga really?"

"Yes really. Now get the fuck outta here." He picked Angela up on his shoulder and slammed the door in my face again. I checked the bag and sure enough, my flatiron was broke. *Oh, it's on.* Does he know how much it cost for a fucking CHI flatiron? It don't matter because once I reveal his secret, Angela won't want him anymore, anyway. *Fucking bastard.*

Tech

I swear on everything, I'm gonna end up killing that bitch Cara. You ever hate someone so bad, that every time you see them, you wanna lay hands on them? It's exactly how I feel about her. See, I've had my eye on Angela for a very long time. I couldn't approach her yet because Marco and I, were traveling a lot, due to our job. Yes, he's the plug and I'm second in command. Do I feel some sorta way about be second? Absolutely not? Marco built this empire on his own. He asked me to join him in the beginning but I was at a hard place in my life, at the time.

My father was dying from prostate cancer and my mom couldn't take it. After he died, a month later, she passed away from a heart attack. It took a toll on me and I disappeared for a year. Marco, knew where I was and came to visit on plenty of occasions. He always said, there's a spot next to him, whenever I'm ready. It took me a while, to take him up on his offer. Now, that I did, I'm as wealthy as he is. Of course, he has more money than me but ain't no complaints over here.

People tend to get jealous when they're not number one in a position like his. I'm the total opposite. I feel, if I wasn't there to put in my sweat and tears, then why would I expect credit for it? However, I may have gotten my spot as second in command but trust, Marco had me doing a lot of shit, to make up for the time missed.

He and I, started opening up business and cleaning money, like most ex dealers and it came with a price in the beginning. We had to pay law enforcement to stay out our business. I hated, they were getting paid for doing nothing but sometimes we have to do shit, we don't want, so it is, what it is.

Back to this bitch Cara though. I met her at a club one night, and she enticed the hell outta me. Her outfit was super tight and short but I knew her and Angela, were friends. Angela, is the one I wanted so I invited Cara to VIP. I started asking questions about her friend and you could see jealousy written all over her face. It didn't matter to me because all I wanted was the number. After a few drinks, she said she'd give it to me, if I helped her to the bathroom. She could barely stand and I'm not gonna let her get hurt because as the owner; I'd have to deal with a lawsuit.

Once I got her to the bathroom, I regretted the shit. I allowed the bitch, to get my jeans down and suck my dick. I'm not gonna lie, she was ok. I already had condoms in my pocket, due to me having eyes on one of the strippers, I had been fucking. Instead of leaving, I fucked the shit outta her. She was screaming and running from the dick. I couldn't even nut because she was too extra. I pulled out and left her right there.

Mind you this was a few weeks ago, which is why, she keeps slick threatening to tell. Angela will probably get mad if she found out but we didn't meet yet. I know how women are though. She'll be mad because of their friendship and say she won't fuck after her. Therefore, I'm not revealing anything and neither is Cara, if I have anything to do with it.

Angela and I, have become very close and I'm mad, I waited so long to link up because she's leaving for school in a few hours. Lucky for me, she's only an hour away. That's nothing and I'll take that drive to see her every day if she wanted. That's how much a nigga was feeling her.

"You are mean." Angela said when I put her down. I stayed the night with her but all we did was talk and kiss, here and there. I respected the hell outta her and didn't wanna come off as only wanting to fuck. However, right before Cara came, she had just gotten out the shower, which is why I opened the door. Now, she got this little ass robe on.

"She's not a real friend Angela." I sat on the bed and pulled her in front of me.

"I keep hearing that."

"Then why are you still fucking with her?"

"We've been around each other for so long, I guess, denial was my best friend."

"Fuck her. She's jealous." I untied her robe and licked my lips. Angela was gorgeous to me. She was darker than what I'm used to but overall, she had the total package. Beauty, brains and common sense.

"Mmmm, Tech." My name sounded sexy as hell coming out her mouth, as I ran my hands up and down her legs and placed kisses on her stomach.

"You want me to stop?"

"Nooooo." My finger went inside her treasure and I could feel her pearl, swelling up.

"Kiss me." I lifted my head and she leaned down to kiss me. Her legs began shaking and so did her body. I pulled my fingers out and replaced them with my mouth.

"Oh fuckkkk." She yelled and grabbed my head. It didn't take long for her to cum in my mouth and more than once. She fell back on the bed when I finished. I let my shorts fall down, lifted her legs and plunged in, before she could protest.

"Mph. Shit woman." I moved in and out and watched her turn my dick white.

"Baby, I'm gonna cum again." I now had her in my arms, against the wall.

"Then do it." I let my lips crash on hers and felt her leaking down my leg.

"Ang, you can't leave."

"I have to Tech. Shit, Oh my Godddddd." She bit down on my neck and shook harder, than a few minutes ago.

"When's the last time you had sex?"

"Last year. I've only done it a few times, with my first sex partner." She whispered in my ear and a nigga was happy, she wasn't a ho. It explained why she kept cumming. I made my way back to the bed, still inside her and laid back. Shorty, went for a ride, I never wanted her to get off of.

"Shit ma." I came so hard, I had to hold her there for a minute.

"You on birth control?"

"No." I lifted her up on my chest.

"I swear, if you weren't going to school, I'd make you keep the baby, I just put inside you. But on the strength of that, we'll go get you a pill to take, before you go to school." She nodded and got up.

"What's wrong?"

"Nothing." She put her robe on and tried to walk past me. I grabbed her wrist.

"Something is wrong."

"You don't want a baby with me? Am I not good enough for you?"

"What the hell? I just said, if you weren't going to school, I'd make you keep it."

"What if I don't wanna take the pill?"

"Shorty, you're confusing me."

"Tech, I know we just met and I promise, I'm not trying to trap you. I don't like taking pills because two of my aunts were addicted to over the counter medicines. I'm talking, Tylenol pm, Nyquil, and Naproxen. I won't even take medication for the migraines, I get because I'm so scared, I'll get addicted and can't stop." I fell back on the bed.

"Damn, shorty. I wish you would've told me that sooner."

"Why, so you didn't have a kid with me?"

"Ma, stop jumping to conclusions. All I'm saying is, I know how excited you are to finish your education. I don't wanna interrupt that and we could've been better prepared. Look." I sat up and made her face me.

70

"I get it, trust me, I do. Let's see what happens and if you are pregnant, we'll go from there. But shorty, I'm telling you right now; you're mine. If you have a kid by me, there's no other men going to be in your life but me."

"Tech, I'm sorry for not telling you. I don't want you to feel like, I trapped you either. I may not take medications but I would've gotten rid of it, if you wanted me too."

"You do know, you would've had to take medicine, to make sure you didn't get an infection?"

"I wouldn't have taken it. If I got one, the hospital would've given me medicine through an IV, like they do when I have migraines."

"You're telling me, you go to the hospital to get medication for headaches?"

"Believe it or not, a lot of people do. Some people can't take medicines through their mouth. I don't tell them, it's because I'm scared of becoming addicted. I just say the Advil isn't working or something. I know, its probably sounding crazy to you and there's no guarantee, I'll even get addicted. However, I'm petrified of the 50%, that I may."

71

"Well, then we have to keep medications away from you and we're gonna have to work on those migraines. Maybe, no sex, is the reason why you get them." She pushed me off her.

"I'm just playing. Look here." I kissed her neck.

"Since, we're not worried about you getting pregnant, let me get some more." She stood up and took her robe back off.

"Then you better come get it. I'm leaving soon." She gestured for me to follow her in the bathroom and me and shorty, did some freaky ass shit to each other. I ain't ever leaving this woman. She just don't know, how stuck she really is.

****

"Shorty, I ain't feeling this." I told Angela as we unpacked her things at school.

"Tech, we haven't been here a full hour and you're already saying, you don't like it." I looked around her room and noticed only one bed.

"Why is it only one bed? Aren't you supposed to have a roommate or some shit?"

"I applied early and they asked if I wanted a roommate and I checked, no. I guess they were able to accommodate me." She shrugged her shoulders and handed me her blanket to put on the bed.

"Oh, so it shouldn't be a problem staying here?" She stopped unpacking and looked at me.

"Tech, one thing I'm not, is a cheater. I know we haven't known each other long, made it official today and now, I'll be away from you." She wrapped her arms around my neck.

"But one thing's for sure and that is, I am officially yours." She pecked my lips.

"You better be. Don't make me come up here and shoot up the place." Her arms dropped and she pushed me back on the bed.

"I see now, you'll need a dose of this good stuff before you leave." She bit down on her lip and my dick sprung straight to life. She was so damn sexy to me.

"Maybe, but don't get mad, if I have you in here screaming."

"How you know, it not what I want?" She removed her clothes and it was on from there. Let's just say, a nigga spent the night. The only reason, I got up this morning is because she had freshman orientation or some shit. Little did she know, I'll be up here a lot more than she think and I wish she would debate it.

Angela

I've been at school now for, four and a half months because I came in the summer. I was missing Tech, like crazy. Don't get me wrong; he visits every weekend but during the week, all I wanted to do was lay under him, after class. We've gotten even closer since the first day, we met.

I learned he's best friends and second in command, with Marco. He actually loved his position and told me, he does almost the same exact thing. He also said, Marco is more reckless than him, but I beg to differ. For example, one day, Tech surprised me during the week and I was coming out of the building with a male student. We were discussing the class and homework. Tech, saw us and almost beat the shit outta dude. Now, the guy won't even look my way. I had to tell him, he has to wait in the room from now on, if he came to surprise me.

Now here it is almost Thanksgiving and I'm going home for the weekend. My mom usually cooks and she invited

Tech to come over. She knew of him but they haven't met, yet. I'm not nervous about them meeting him. Its actually vice versa. Tech said, he's never met a chicks' parents and didn't know how he should act in front of them. No idea, why he was nervous. It's going to be funny watching him sweat, tho.

"What's up bitchhhhhhh?" I yelled in the phone to Rakia, who just called. She had been working her ass off in college and wasn't going to come home, until I told her, she could stay with me.

"Nothing. I was calling to see if you needed a ride home. I can scoop you up on the way to Jersey."

"Tech, is coming but I'll tell him never mind. You ok?" She sounded upset over the phone.

"Yea."

"You don't sound it. What's going on?"

"Cara, called to tell me, she heard Bobbi and Marco, were expecting." I swear, her cousin was like a damn disease. Granted, I played a part in her evilness but she was literally still out to hurt Rakia, even in college. You would think with Rakia being gone, it would make her stop competing but she called, with the dumbest reasons and would always tell her negative shit about Marco.

"Rak, stop letting her upset you."

"I know Marco and I, were never a couple or anything like that but I guess, it's hard to get over your first crush."

"Awwww. You had your first crush with Marco." She sucked her teeth.

"Look. There's no telling if she's lying or not. And who cares, if he is expecting with her? Once he sees you, he'll push her to the side anyway." She told me Marco called her one day and asked if they could still be friends. Don't even ask how he got her number because she said, they were never able to exchange them, the day at the block party. She accepted his apology and they speak a lot, well spoke a lot because Rakia will block him quick.

"I can't compete with a baby."

"Well fuck him then. Didn't you say, they're some fine men up there?" She started laughing.

"Ok, then take one of them up on their offer and go on a date. See how it goes and base your decision off that."

"I guess. Look, I have to finish this assignment. I'll see you in a few days."

"Ok. And don't worry about Cara. She is the devil and looking to hurt you. It took me a while to see it but she's jealous of the both of us."

"I'll talk to you later." She hung up and I looked up at the television to finish watching my show. Rakia may not say nothing to Cara but you bet, I will.

****

"Damn, I didn't think you would ever get here." Rakia, stared at me and smiled.

"Does he know?"

"Know what?" We put my bags in the trunk and sat inside. It was chilly as hell out.

"Don't play me. It's all over your face and right here." She pointed to the pouch in my stomach.

After the first day, Tech and I, had sex, we started using condoms, just in case he didn't get me pregnant, which was fine with me. I'm actually the one who encouraged it. Every time he came to spend the weekend with me, we'd fuck like rabbits. I didn't have morning sickness right away, therefore; I assumed, there was no baby. It wasn't until, two months later, when it dawned on me, I hadn't gotten a period. I went to the store, picked up a few tests, took them and sure enough, my ass was expecting. I thought about terminating it but it wouldn't be fair to him.

I went to the doctors at an Urgent Care facility and once she confirmed the pregnancy and gave me the prescription for prenatal vitamins, I had to sit her down and explain, I didn't do pills. She assured me, that in no shape, or form, could anyone get addicted to vitamins. Taking her word for it, I've been swallowing them faithfully and at the last appointment, she said I was exactly sixteen weeks and the baby was healthy. Now, all I have to do is tell him and my parents. They're gonna be upset but he's gonna be happy as hell. We've talked about having kids, once I graduate. Looks like, we'll get our wish sooner, then later. I hope he's ready because I damn sure ain't.

"No, he doesn't and neither do my parents, so keep your lips sealed."

"Angela, you have to eventually tell them."

"I will, after the holiday. My parents should meet him first and see how much we love each other."

"Oh shit. You're in love?"

"Yes. We confessed it to each other, last week. Actually, he said it first."

"Awwww, that's so cute. I can't wait to be in love. I mean, I think Marco is my first love but then again, we didn't do anything but kiss. He did track me down at the block party and then again, at school. You think he loves me?" I shook my head laughing at her ramble on. She is such an amazing person, with a great heart. I don't know how, I let Cara talk me into treating her like shit.

For the rest of the ride, we talked about everything under the sun. It didn't even dawn on me, that Tech hadn't called. He's usually checking in, every chance he gets. I guess, he was busy and I didn't wanna disturb him. I'm not naïve, to the life he leads and I refuse to be one of those chicks, who start a relationship off not trusting my man. If I did, what's the use of being in one?

By the time Rakia pulled up, it was after six and dark as hell outside. My dad came out to help with the bags and my mom was inside, getting the turkey ready for tomorrow. I could smell some of the food cooking and my stomach rumbled. When we walked in, Tech was sitting in the living room watching television. I ran over and kissed him. The way he made my body feel, just by touching me, had me ready to ask if we could go to his place. I was super horny and he knew it too.

"I'ma tear it up later." He kissed my lips.

"What are you doing here?"

"Well, he came to introduce himself and has been here waiting for you."

"REALLY! I thought you were working, that's why I didn't call you."

"I don't care where I'm at. If you wanna talk, hit my line and I'll stop whatever I'm doing, to give you my full attention." I wrapped my arms around his neck and kissed him. I really was in love with this man. Rakia came in, clearing her throat.

"Hey Rak. Have you seen my boy?" After she hugged him, and said no, she left us standing there. I told him what Cara did and he was angrier, than I thought he should be. Maybe because it's his brother.

"Your mom wants you." My dad said and passed Tech, a beer. I removed my jacket and walked in the kitchen.

"Hey mommy." I went to hug her.

"Got dammit, Angela." I backed up. I didn't knock anything over, so why was she yelling?

"What's wrong?" She wiped her hands on the apron and smacked fire from my ass. The shit was so loud, I know Tech would be here in a second and sure enough, he was.

"Yo, what was that?" He stood in front of me.

"You bring your ass up in my house, introducing yourself as this perfect gentleman, knowing the entire time, she's pregnant." He turned to look at me. *How the hell did she know and I hadn't said anything?*

"You pregnant?" He asked and I was wondering why my dad hadn't come in the kitchen. Then again, he's used to us arguing. It's been a long time, since she's hit me.

My mom hated me because my dad cheated on her and had me, with another woman. My birth mother died in a car accident, which forced her to raise me. She didn't start acting mean until, I was in high school. It's probably because my dad, would often say, I resembled my mom. I blame her for me, treating Rakia, the way I did. I needed to take my anger out on someone else and she always felt the brunt of it.

"I was gonna tell you this weekend as a surprise." I had tears running down my face.

"You knew she was pregnant and put your hands on her anyway." He had Sally, by the shirt and backed up against the wall.

"I don't know what type of shit you on but make that the last time, you lay hands on my girl. Matter of fact, get your shit. Ain't no way in hell, I'm letting you stay here." He grabbed my hand.

"I can't leave Rakia."

"Yo, Rak." He shouted up the steps. She came down with a surprised look.

"Get your stuff, we're leaving."

83

"Ugh ok." She ran and grabbed her things.

"Daddy, I'll see you later."

"Let me know where you are." He stood up and came over to me.

"I'm sorry, she hit you and baby, if I could lay her on her ass, trust me, I would."

"GET OUT MY HOUSE!" She yelled. Tech squeezed my hand and I had to ask him to calm down.

"I love you daddy."

"Bye." Rakia spoke to both of them.

"Rakia, you can stay with us at my place or get a hotel. It's up to you." Tech told her when we got outside.

"Maybe, I'll just go to my grandparents."

"No. You'll be miserable. Listen." I walked over to her.

"Tech has a huge house and I promise not to be loud, if we, you know. I won't feel comfortable, if you stay in a hotel. Please come with us." I whined and she gave in. Tech had her follow us in his truck, that I didn't notice was there when we arrived because it was on the other side of the street.

"I'm happy, you're gonna have my kid." He kissed my hand and drove to his house. Marco called and asked if he could meet him later. It didn't bother me. Rakia was with me, so I wouldn't be alone. After he dropped me off and we got comfortable, Rakia and I, fell asleep on the couch.

I don't know what time he came home but felt him lifting me up and opened my eyes. He had a blanket on Rak and turned the alarm on. He took me upstairs and laid me in the bed. I waited for him to get out the shower and heard his phone go off. I figured it was Marco again, so I answered it. The caller never said a word. I looked down at the number and it was unknown. The person hung up and called back. Of course, I answered again and the person never spoke

"I can hear you breathing. If you wanna talk to him, just ask."

"Fuck you bitch." The chick said and hung up. I was wondering if, I should mention it, however, when he emerged from the bathroom, the water was still clinging to his skin. The only thing on my mind at the time, was him entering me.

"You got pregnant the first time we had sex, didn't you?" I nodded my head yes and watched him place kisses on my belly.

"That makes you about four months."

"Yessssss." He slid his tongue in between my legs and whatever he mentioned afterwards, was a blur. Right now, it's all about me. He took my body to places, it surely missed. I'll ask him about the phone call another time.

Rakia

I loved the relationship, Tech and Angela had. I pray he's not cheating on her, because I don't think she'd be able to take it. After being around her and speaking on the phone all the time, I've learned that she has a good heart too. Some people may not agree to me, agreeing to a friendship but its my choice and no one else's. Hell, some people will continue to be friends with people who slept with their baby daddy.

This morning when I woke up, of course, she wasn't at the other end of the couch. I didn't expect her to be; especially since the two of them hadn't seen each other in almost a week. Yea, he went every weekend to see her but this past weekend she asked him not to, because school was out Tuesday and it was no need, when they'd be together for the next few days.

I was on my way out the door to go see my grandparents, when Angela came down the steps, calling my name. Say what you want but I don't hold grudges against anyone, even though, I should. Plus, I'm going, in hopes of seeing my parents. They may not have been stable in my life, but we do speak. It's when I ask them to get clean, that they push me away. No one wants their parents to be on drugs but I've accepted it and only hope, they get better before it's too late.

I saw a few hickeys on Angela's neck and shook my head. Those two could never keep their hands to themselves. I waited for her to come closer and she pushed me out the door. I wasn't sure why, until I saw tears falling down her face. I hit the alarm on my truck and hurried to get in, like I was in trouble or something. She asked me to hurry up and pull off, before Tech realized she was gone. I decided against asking why she was upset because when people are hurting, they'll speak on it, when they're ready.

"Yea, Tech." She answered the phone after it rang five different times. She kept sending it to voicemail.

"I left with Rak. I'm fine Tech." She wiped her eyes and continued talking.

"I'll see you later." She hung up and shut her phone off. *What the hell was going on?* I pulled up in front of my

88

grandparents' house and it was a few people out there;
including Cara. My grandmother always had our entire family
over for the holidays and the little bit of people here now, will
soon turn into more and a street party. I usually never entertain
anyone and stay upstairs but not this year.

"Rak, I think he's cheating." She said and stared out the
window.

"Ang, I find that hard to believe. You two are always
together and everyone, and I do mean everyone, knows you
two are a couple. What makes you think that?" She explained
about the phone call last night and I can't front. It did look
shady as hell for a woman to call twice and then curse her out.
Like if the man is cheating, why take it out on the woman, who
most likely has no clue?

"Ang, I've never been in a relationship. So, I can't tell
you what to do. I am gonna ask if you spoke to him about it?"

"For what, Rak? He'll just deny it and right now, I
can't take any more hurt. My mom smacked the shit outta me
and told me to never come back. After speaking to my dad,
I've come to the realization, he's not going to leave her, which

means, I will no longer be daddy's girl and now this shit with

Tech. I swear, if I could smoke a blunt right now, I would."

KNOCK! KNOCK! I heard on my window and looked,

to see my childish ass cousin, Rahmel. He's twenty going back

to the age of six. He's probably the only one, I got along with

the most. He wouldn't let anyone fuck with me, especially;

Cara when he was around. It was when he wasn't, that she tries.

Yes, he's her brother but the two of them, are like oil and milk.

He calls her all types of hoes and a wanna be, a baller bitch.

Actually, it's pretty funny to watch them argue. I let the

window down.

"Hey cuz. I see you came home to eat, with your

greedy ass. Open the door." I unlocked it and he slid in the

backseat.

"What up Ang. Y'all smoking or what?" He lifted the

blunt from behind his ear. Yes, I indulged once in a blue moon

and I mean the moon had to be dark blue, for me to smoke.

"No thanks Rahmel." Ang pulled the visor down to

make sure she looked ok and opened her door.

"I'm staying in cuz. Everybody be tryna smoke and don't wanna put in on shit. Fuck that." I shook my head and he hopped out and sat in the front seat.

Ang and I, walked up to the porch and my aunt Shanta, came running over to hug me. My aunt may be a beggar but she has never looked like one. Her clothes, hair, nails and even house, stayed on point. I really did love her but I knew she had Cara, who hated me and had to keep her love for me, hidden at times. I know it sounds crazy but its been plenty of days, Cara threw bitch fits because she'd do something for me.

I noticed Cara, coming out the door and her face turned up when she saw us. How could someone hate you so much and you've never done a thing to them? I use to try and figure it out, but I stopped worrying about it. I spoke and went inside the house.

My grandmother was in the kitchen cooking and my grandfather, had his lazy ass on the couch with a beer watching television. These two make me sick and the only reason I halfway respect them, is because they took me in. Unfortunately, it was for the money but I'm sure there are people out there, going through the same thing and suffering far worse. I spoke to them and went to my old room. Nothing was touched and my sheets and comforter, must've just been clean because they had the Gain laundry detergent smell. I closed the door and Angela laid on the bed. I asked if she needed anything and all she wanted to do, is sleep. It's to be expected, since she's expecting.

I left her alone and decide to log onto the laptop, the school purchased for me and look on Instagram. Celebrities were posting videos with their families and so were people from the area. I didn't have too many following me, but if their page was opened, I surveyed it, to be nosy. I wanted so bad to look on the chick Bobbi's page but she was private. Maybe, its for the better. I heard a knock on my door and opened it. My grandmother stood there with an envelope in her hand. She looked behind her and closed it.

"What? She pregnant?" She pointed to Ang, who was sleeping. I nodded.

"At least, it's by a nigga who can take care of her and the baby." My grandmother knew all the gossip. I'm shocked she knew about Tech, but hey, people talk.

"Anyway, sit down." She pointed to one of the folding chairs I had in my room. I kept one in there to use, when I wanted to read. Sitting in bed, tends to make a person tired and sometimes, I'd be ready to go to sleep at six o'clock.

"Here." She handed me the envelope and my eyes grew big.

"Grandma, where did you get this kind of money?" It was a check for seventy thousand dollars, written out to me.

"Listen Rakia. I know we were hard on you growing up but it wasn't to be mean." I looked up at her.

"I was getting you ready for these tough streets out here. You know, you were born touched." I sucked my teeth.

"Watch it girl."

"Like I was saying. You're special and I knew the kids would give you a hard time, especially; the damn demon child, Cara." I nodded.

"I had to make sure you would grow up, never depending on a man, for anything. It may not have been right in your eyes, but it's the only way I knew how to make you have tough skin. Anyway, I've been saving $322 the state gave me every month, for the last eighteen years. This check may not be a lot but it's the reason, I worked under the table. Your parents couldn't provide for you, and I didn't want to use the money on anything because it was yours. I kept it in an account all these years and never spent a dime. If you do the calculations, its more than what they gave but it's because of the interest." I started crying.

"Rakia, I apologize for making you feel like you weren't good enough but I always knew you'd be special and not in the way you think." She lifted my face.

"Baby, you have a gift and I'm so happy, you got outta here to pursue your dreams. Shit, it's nothing here but trouble and heartache. All I ask is, you finish your education and spend this money, any way you want. I know you wanted to get a new phone and now you can. Buy a new wardrobe, do whatever you want with it. It's your money but please finish your education and make something of yourself. Lord knows, that ho ass, thot, granddaughter of mine, ain't gonna do shit with her life." I busted out laughing and I turned to see Angela doing the same.

"I love you grandma and I'm glad you explained why you were so mean. I thought no one loved me." She sat on the bed.

"Rakia, you are my flesh and blood. Your grandfather and I, love you very much. It may not have seemed that way and again, we apologize but people don't always use their words to say it." She stared at me and smiled.

"I wish your parents could've raised you but we can't always have what we want."

"But why couldn't they get off drugs and raise me?"

"Honey, don't ever think, they didn't want to be around you. They stayed away to keep others from laughing at you. I know you didn't care but as parents, we protect our kids from as much, as we can."

"I guess."

"At least, they came to every graduation, plays and all the other activities you were in." She was right. Anything I was involved in, my parents showed up. They would stay in the back but always made sure, I saw them. I nodded and stood to give her a hug.

"What's going on in here?"

"I didn't lock the door?" My grandmother questioned Cara, when she busted in. I hurried and put the check in my pocket.

"Oh, you did. I used the butter knife to open it." She shrugged her shoulders like it was ok.

"I swear, your mother dropped you a hundred times, when you were a baby."

"At least, I didn't come out retarded like her." My grandmother smacked her so hard, she fell against the wall.

"All these years, I've watched and listened to you disrespect her, in front of your friends and people we didn't know. You did all that and she is still on top of the world. You should learn from "*the special one,*" as you all call her. She can teach you a few things."

"RAKIA!" I heard my grandfather yelling as he came up the steps.

"What's wrong?"

"You need to get that nigga outside, before he kills Rahmel." I ran over to the window and couldn't believe my eyes. Marco, had a gun in Rahmel's face and no one was moving.

"Did you fuck him?" Cara had the nerve to ask.

"No and I don't know why he's doing that." I ran down the steps and out the door.

"MARCO!" I screamed and he didn't move. I made my way over to him and stood in front of Rahmel.

"What the fuck Rakia? You fucking this nigga."

"Marco, he's my cousin." He stared at me, shrugged his shoulders and put the gun in his waist.

"What up though? Why you ain't tell me you came to town?" Did this man, just pull a gun on my cousin and then act like nothing happened? He really is crazy.

"Yo, cuz. I don't know what you did to him but I won't drive your truck anymore." He handed me the keys and walked off. Marco didn't apologize or anything. I didn't know my cousin went anywhere in my truck but Marco must've seen him and flipped. But why? We're not a couple.

"What do you want Marco?" I tried to leave but he wouldn't let me. I saw all my family members standing out there watching.

"You know, what I want."

"I'm sorry, I can't give you that." The last conversation we had, he asked me to be his woman and I declined. We lived hours away and after the shit Cara put in my head, I couldn't trust him. It's not his fault but I was scared to get hurt.

"Why not Rak? What the fuck, yo?" I smiled as he said the nickname he gave me. He said Rakia is cute but corny and he liked Rak, better.

"That's why Marco." I pointed to Rahmel on the porch.

"You pulled a weapon on my cousin and pretended like it was ok. Then, you still have this chick following you around." I noticed the Bobbi chick, who had gotten out her car and was on her way over to us. He looked at one of his guards and she stopped in her tracks.

"Marco, we're not good for each other and you know it. You said at the block party, that you have the ability to hurt me bad."

"Rak, I wouldn't though."

"Marco, I'm different and not the type of woman, you're used to dealing with." He pulled me in close.

"You are different and very special to me. It's the exact reason, I want you. You won't take my shit. Ma, I need you in my life, to keep me grounded. I promise, I won't hurt you." I stood on my tippy toes and pecked his lips.

"I can't take the chance Marco. I don't know, if I'll be able to survive a heartbreak. I may be a genius and book smart but loving a man, is not something, I'm an expertise in. We can still be friends."

"Nah. I'm not gonna believe you don't want me, the same way I want you. I'll give you a little more time but when I come, I'm not taking no for an answer."

"Marco." He turned to walk away. I tried to go after him but the guards blocked me. I don't know why I started crying but I did.

99

"I guess, he told your special ass, your services were no longer needed." I pushed past Cara and went upstairs.

"You ok?" Angela asked and I laid on the bed.

"I'm stuck. I want him so bad Ang, but I'm scared. I don't know how to fight and what if his chick comes back around? Do you know she followed him here?"

"She's a stalker, for real."

"Yea. I don't know what to do with a man like him. Maybe Cara's right."

"About?"

"About me finding someone as special as me. You know, someone more of my speed."

"Rak, its obvious you're fine enough, for a man like Marco, to want you. I understand you're scared and you have every right to be. Look at what, I'm going through with Tech and who knows, if he's really cheating? I get it Rak but you can't be scared forever. You have to take that leap, and experience, is always the best teacher." I nodded and turned on my side. Could I take a leap of faith with him? Should I?

Instead of going downstairs with everyone else, we stayed in the room, until it was time to eat. After we finished, she asked to stay the night over here. I guess, once my grandmother came up and revealed all the things she did, she felt comfortable being here. I know, I did. I wanted to call Marco but shut my phone off, to avoid temptation. We both needed to think about what we really wanted.

Marco

A nigga was hurt, by Rakia rejecting me. I've never in my life, had any woman tell me no. Shit, I'm Marco Santiago. The motherfucking nigga. I could get anyone, I wanted. However, the only person I wanted, was Rakia Winters. It's like my body and soul craved her. I needed to speak with her every morning, throughout the day and before I went to sleep. Don't ask me what she did because a nigga couldn't tell you. Maybe, it's because she didn't take my shit and we'd have real deep conversations, who knows. All I know, is she belonged to me and anyone who thought different, would deal with me.

When I saw her truck pass me on the highway, I knew it was hers, by the Harvard sticker on the back. The nigga driving wasn't anyone I knew and thought maybe it was stolen. But then, what if it's some nigga she fucking? All types of thoughts ran through my head. Sad to say, I followed it, yanked his ass out the truck and put a gun to his head.

Once Rak, told me who he was, I let him go. She had the nerve to get upset, over me not giving a fuck. She should know by now, how I am. We spoke all the time and she's even been on the phone a few times, as I handled business. Maybe seeing it, is different. I heard her call my name as I walked away but I had to get away from her and see what this stupid bitch was doing here. I didn't want her trying to fight Rakia, like she promised to do, whenever she saw her. I had Bobbi follow me and pulled over on the side of the road. It was pretty dark and she was nervous to step out the car and she should be.

"Why you following me?"

"Marco, what is it about her, Huh? You speak to her all day long and we don't even talk that much. I mean, we can finish having sex and if she calls, you'll leave the room to talk and dare me to say something. Is her pussy better than mine? Does she suck you off better? What is it?" I shook my head listening to herself, try and compare to Rakia. The sad part is, she couldn't. Of course, I wanted Rakia sexually but mentally, she had my mind, gone. I can't explain the feelings and didn't care to.

"She'll never be a concern of yours. As far as, who I spend my days talking to, the time I'm spending with them or anything else, I do. I suggest you keep the questions to yourself and if you ever follow me again, you'll regret knowing that side of me." I nodded to my guard and he drug her by the hair and back to her car. It may have been extreme; however, she needed to know, a nigga meant every word.

****

"Shit is lit, tonight." I said to Tech, who's been going through some shit with his girl. Evidently, on Thanksgiving, she bounced with Rakia and didn't come home, until the next day. Then when she was there, she kept giving him the cold shoulder and one word answers, to his questions. He couldn't for the life of him, figure out what her problem was. I asked if she knew about Cara and he said no. If she did, he doesn't see her holding in that type of information.

Oh, we both knew how Cara was. She wanted to catch a baller so bad, she tried her hand and all my niggas; including Tech. I hadn't told anyone about the two days in New York with her because not only was I embarrassed but felt like, she wasn't worth discussing. Unfortunately, my boy got caught up, in her web of shit. He may not have been with Angela but she's definitely gonna see everything wrong with it.

"Yea, it is. Have you spoken to Rakia?"

"Nah. She's right. I'm not ready for her." I shrugged it off and almost spilled my drink, when I noticed her walk in with Angela and Cara. They were both going back to school tomorrow and here they are, out and about. What the hell were they doing here and with her?

"Yo, there's your woman." He stood up and shook his head. Neither of us, went to them. I think we were both low-key nervous about Cara shouting us out.

"Can we dance for y'all?"

"Nah, we good." I walked off to use the bathroom. When I came out the stall, this stupid bitch was standing there with her arms folded.

"Marco, why are you treating me like shit? I thought we had a good time in New York." I didn't respond and continued washing my hands.

"Marco, I love you and I know you feel the same." I laughed so hard, I had to hold my stomach. This bitch is delusional and needs her head checked.

"Move Cara." She stood in front of the door.

"Why?"

"Because I don't want you."

"But you let me suck your dick a few times and.-"

"SO, THE FUCK WHAT BITCH." I tossed her to the side.

"Plenty of bitches suck my dick and what? You think you're special? You on some stalking shit and you didn't even get fucked." I couldn't believe she came in here, talking this dumb shit.

"Marco, how you gonna be with my cousin though?"

"Your cousin?" Now I was confused.

"Rakia Winters."

"Y'all not related."

"Yes, we are. My mom and her father, are brother and sister." I ran my hand down my face. How come I didn't know that? Granted they were around each other but I assumed they were friends like her and Angela.

"How do you think she'd feel, knowing I sucked you off."

"It was way before her."

"She doesn't know that and trust me, she'll believe me over you." She smirked. This bitch is looney as hell. Could I risk her telling? I could just kill her but then Rakia would be upset. I don't for the life of me, understand why she doesn't hate this bitch.

"I'll be in touch."

"I don't know what for?"

"Oh, for my silence." I couldn't hold it in any longer and my hands were around her throat.

"If you say one word to her, I'll fucking kill you. Do you understand me?" Her eyes were bulging out.

"I can't fucking hear you." She tried her best to nod yes. I squeezed a little harder and slammed her dumb ass on the ground. The back of her head hit the floor and somehow, her nose started bleeding.

"You got me fucked up, if you think, I'm about to play some blackmailing game with you." She didn't say anything because she was trying to catch her breath.

"Remember what I said." I gave her a powerful kick to her stomach. She's not about to fuck up anything, I was working for, in order to get Rakia. I stepped over her and walked out the bathroom door. I noticed Angela upstairs with Tech and Rakia, on the dancefloor. I made my way over and grinded behind her. I'm not a dancer but I had a few moves.

"You smell good." I sniffed her neck.

"So do you." She wrapped her arms around my neck and threw her tongue in my mouth. Usually, I don't show public affection but like I said, shorty had me gone, when it came to her.

"Mmmmm, I missed you." She said and I got all fuzzy inside.

"Rakia." She put her fingers to my lips and said she was ready to go. Now, why would I keep talking when she said that? I grabbed her hand and we were on our way out the door.

"Oh my God, Cara! What happened to you?" She was bent over a bar stool. I swear, this bitch in front of us, be doing the most. She pointed at me and as usual, I shrugged my shoulders.

"Marco, please tell me you didn't do this."

"Nah, I did. Come on." I tried to leave and she let go of my hand.

"Why would you do this?"

"You want me to tell her?" Cara said and smirked.

"This bitch cornered me in the bathroom and said she wanted to hurt you."

"The bathroom? Why was she in there with you?"

"Because the bitch is crazy. Like I was saying. I told her, if she laid hands on you, that's her ass. And well, she threatened to do it anyway so I had to show her, I meant business. You ready now?" She folded her arms.

"Hurt me. How could she hurt me?"

"Rakia, last year when.-" She tried to say and lucky for me, gunshots rang out. After we got up, I snatched her and took her to my car.

"Put me down." I sat her inside and ran back to the club to make sure, Tech and his girl was ok. Once I found them and they were fine, I went back to see my car door was open and Rakia was gone. *DAMN!* I can't win for losing with her.

****

"You ok?" I heard Tech asking Ang, when I walked back in. I didn't see Rakia, so I assumed she left.

"Yea, I'm fine. Where's Rak?" I explained what went down and she sucked her teeth. We all witnessed the great lengths, Cara was going through to fuck with Rakia.

"Who the fuck would shoot shit up? We ain't beefing with no one." I was pissed. Not only were our women there. Yea I claimed Rak. Not only were our women there, but so were innocent bystanders. In my line of work, I've always been extra careful, not to involve outsiders.

"GET THESE MOTHERFUCKERS OUTTA HERE!" Tech shouted and the bouncers scrambled to remove the crowd. One guy, in particular stood there staring at me and I had no idea who he was. Me, being the man I am, strolled down the steps to find out, what's up. If this nigga is bold enough to

110

stare and hold his spot, then I'm gonna see what's up? In my eyes, I felt challenged and a nigga hated that. I didn't request an audience, nor did I want my guards to follow.

"You know me bro?" I stood there with my arms folded.

"I ain't your fucking bro." I chuckled in his face.

"Nah, you right. But check this. My brother told everyone to leave; yet, you're still standing here. Do we have a motherfucking problem?"

"As a matter of fact, we do."

"Oh yea." Tech said coming up behind me.

"Your boy here, can't seem to understand, what everybody out means."

"BOY!"

"Yea boy." He took a step forward and I laid his ass, the fuck out. I'm talking, I put his ass to sleep.

"We got a problem?" I asked the guys who came in his defense. It was at least ten of them. How the fuck are they in the club, if Tech told everyone to leave?

"We good." One of the dudes said and they helped the person up and left.

"Yo. What the hell?" We stayed at the club a little longer and waited for the cops to tell us everything was clear. Luckily, no one was hit and only a few bottles and glasses were spread out on the floor.

"What's up ma?" I spoke in my phone. It rang a few times but I kept ignoring it because we were tryna figure shit out.

"I need to see you."

"You got that. Show up at this address in an hour." I hung up and sent her the address to my mansion, out in the Palisades. Yea, I have a few cribs in the area but the one she's going to, a woman has never seen, unless she was a family member. I told Tech we'd hook up tomorrow and jumped in my car.

By the time, I got home, it gave me enough time to shower and get comfortable. I'm sure she had mad questions, so I'm anticipating a long night.

Rakia

"Are you ok Cara?" I left the car, Marco put me in, when I noticed her struggling to come out the door.

"Take me to the hospital please?" She practically begged. I helped her get in the truck and sped off. It wasn't far away and I needed to make sure she was ok, so I could meet with Marco. I needed to know what the hell was going on between the two of them. Why did he say, she was trying to hurt me? What was she trying to tell me? My head was hurting from trying to figure it out.

"What happened to her?" One of the nurses, asked when we stepped in,

"Her boyfriend beat me up in the club." I looked at this bitch like she was crazy. Did she really blame Marco? I mean, he did do it but Rahmel said, there's a no telling rule in the streets.

"I think my ribs are broken and I may have a concussion." Oh, she was milking the shit out of this.

"Ma'am, I'm gonna have to call the police. I suggest you speak to your boyfriend and ask him to turn himself in."

"Wait! You don't even know if he did this? She could be lying?" It was at this very moment, I knew for sure, my own flesh and blood hated me.

"GET THE FUCK OUT RAKIA!" She screamed and I backed up. She may have called me names but never, did she scream at me.

"HOW COULD YOU TAKE HIS SIDE OVER MINE?" I ran out the hospital and to my car. My hands were shaking and I was trying to remain calm. I called Marco and asked if we could meet. He gave me the address to some place that was forty minutes away. I waited a few minutes and once I calmed down, I drove to the destination.

When I got there, I re-checked the address to make sure, this was the right place. I mean, it had big, black iron gates and security was sitting in a booth. He took my name and pressed a button for them to open. He told me to follow the long driveway and the house was in the back. I'm not exaggerating when I say, the house was a mansion. It had to be at least ten bedrooms in here. There were a few cars in front of the three-car garage and let's not even discuss the flowers and grass. Everything outside was beautiful. I can't even imagine what the inside looked like.

I opened my car door and stepped out, only to see him standing in the doorway, shirtless in a pair of basketball shorts. *Lord, help me not bring out my inner hoe.* Making my way to the door, my phone rang and it was Ang, asking if I were ok. Once I told her, where I was, she started screaming and telling me to rock his world, whatever that meant. Excuse me, but I'm not familiar with all the slang. Like I said, my ass wasn't very social so when people discussed certain things, if I didn't understand them, I'd walk away; unless it was a teacher talking about school work.

"You ok?" He pulled me in and wiped my eyes.

"Marco, what happened? Cara, said you beat her up. I mean, I know you did something. Then, we get to the hospital and she told the people, it was you who did it. I tried to defend you and say she was lying but she screamed at me to leave and accused me of taking your side. What is going on?"

"Calm down Rak. You're scared, shaking and making me upset. When I get upset, it's not something you wanna see."

"Are you threatening to hurt me?" He laughed.

"No. I could never hurt you. Come on." He led me up the steps and I stopped, to take my shoes off. The floors were so nice, I didn't wanna scratch them up.

"Here?" He handed me a towel, washcloth and some of his clothes.

"Are you saying, I'm dirty?" I dropped my shoes and phone.

"No, but you have mascara running down your face, your dress has a tear in it, and I can see, sweat beads on your forehead. If you wanna talk to me, I need you to be relaxed." I stared at him and wondered how he could do something so vicious to Cara and be so nice to me? Nice people, don't hurt anyone. *Right?*

"You need help?" I must've been staring too long.

"Ummm. No. Direct me to the shower." He showed it to me and passed me some pear soap and lotion, for when I finished.

"My mom uses it, when she stays here." He laughed and closed the door on his way out. I glanced around and even the bathroom, was gorgeous. Too be honest, my ass was scared to touch anything.

Oh my God, this shower is the best one I ever had. The water came out of different shower heads and they all hit certain spots. When I got out, I wrapped the towel around me and sat on the vanity type chair, he had in here to apply the lotion. I washed my face and brushed my teeth with the extra one, he had to have brought in, while I was in here.

"Nah, don't kill her but let her know, she better recant her story, or I'll make sure.-" He turned around and hung the phone up. I was scared to ask him anything, after hearing him say those words. I'm positive he was speaking of Cara.

"You look good in anything you wear." His tongue slid over his lips and my body reacted in a way, I never felt.

"Thank you. Can I sit on the bed?"

"Ma, this is my castle and anytime you're here, consider it yours too. You can do whatever you want and I do mean whatever." He stood in front of me and helped me on the bed because it was extra high off the ground.

"Oh my God, it's so soft." I fell back and a few seconds later, he was on top, staring at me. I jumped and he held me there.

"Rakia, I would never violate you. I just wanted to lay on top of you. If you want me to get up, I will."

"Noooo. No, you're fine. I've never had a man this close to me." He smirked.

"Are you a virgin?"

"Ummm. No. Wait! If I do myself, does that count?"

"What you mean?" He pulled me up by the arms and sat next to me.

"Don't laugh when I tell you. It's so embarrassing." I covered my face. He moved my hands and told me to continue.

"The day, I saw you at the bodega, it was love at first sight for me." He smiled and moved my hair out my face.

"I went home and asked my aunt for some money. She asked me what for and I told her, to buy female items and she handed over a hundred dollars. Anyway, I took a bus to the mall, went into one of the freaky stores and brought a toy."

"Word?" It's like he couldn't believe it.

"Yea. I paid for one and hid it in my purse. Well that night, I showered, locked my bedroom door and thought about you. I put the toy in my, you know."

"Pussy."

"Yes."

"Baby, don't ever be afraid to talk about your body. It's beautiful and you should embrace everything about it." I smiled.

"I placed the toy at my opening and went in slow. The porn sites for virgins say, it hurts the first time so it made me extremely nervous. Unfortunately, my grandfather banged on the door, looking for the iron and scared the daylights outta me. I rammed it inside by accident." He now covered his mouth laughing.

"You're not supposed to laugh."

"I'm sorry." He pecked my lips and sat against the headboard listening.

"I hid it under the covers and jumped up, to pass it to him. I locked my door back and went to get the toy. It had blood on it so I threw it in the trash. Needless to say, that's the only time, I had sex." I put both of my hands on my face again.

"Am I a virgin?"

"If the only thing that penetrated you, is the toy, I'd say you were." He stood up and pulled me with him.

"I mean, you never had a man, kiss on your neck, like this." His lips touched my neck and then, my shoulder blade, right before he removed my shirt.

"You've never had a man, caress these pretty ass tities, or suck on them." He turned me around and sat me on the bed. I felt his mouth on my breasts and the feeling in between my legs, returned.

"Lift up ma." I did what he said and watched as my shorts were taken off. I tried to grab the covers but he pushed them away.

"Damn, I knew you were beautiful but your body is fucking perfect and I'm the only one who's ever touched it. Yea, you're mine from here on out."

120

"Marco." I sat up on my elbows to say something and outta nowhere, he lifted my legs, spread them apart and his mouth and tongue, had me screaming and grabbing the comforter.

"You ready?" He asked and I had no idea what he was talking about.

"Yesssss." I arched my back when his finger went inside and my body shook, uncontrollably. Whatever he did, it felt like the blood was rushing from my brain and it wouldn't stop. My heart was racing and my toes were curling. Something leaked out and I was ready to pass out.

"Nah, ma. Your man, needs you."

"Marco, I'm scared." He laid on top of me.

"If you want me to stop, I will. If you want me to keep going, I promise to make you feel good." I bit down on my lip and nodded my head yes. I tried to cover my face but he stopped me, by kissing me passionately.

"Its gonna hurt." He whispered in my ear and I dug my nails far in his back, as he pushed his way in.

"You feel that?"

"What, it hurting?"

"I just broke your hymen, so you were a virgin. Whatever you did, never broke it." He moved in and out, making the pain turn into pleasure.

"Shit, I ain't never leaving you." He said and began kissing me again. I could hear a smacking noise down below and instantly became embarrassed.

"It's fine Rak." He lifted both of my arms, over my head and attacked my neck. My body had a mind of its own and started grinding under him.

"There you go ma." He continued pleasing me.

"Here, try it on top." He laid on his back and showed me how to mount him. After, he mentioned what to do, it was on from there.

"Got damn Rak, this is some good ass pussy. Ride it faster." He lifted me up and had me drop harder, until I started doing it on my own.

"Ahhhhhh shit. I'm cumming ma." He placed his thumb on my nub and rubbed, until we came together. I thought we were done, but he had me, with my ass in the air,

122

my body leaning over the bed, sitting on the dresser and any other position possible. I can't tell you how long we had sex but it was definitely, a long time.

"It hurts Marco." I told him in the shower. He took his time washing me up and had me wait, while he changed the sheets. Once he finished, I climbed in with him and he pulled me close.

"You're my woman now, and no one is gonna ever hurt you again." I turned over to face him.

"I'm nervous about being your woman."

"Why?"

"Marco, there's some things, I have to tell you.

"Ma, I know about your anxiety issues, the medicine you take, where you attend school, how much money is in the check your grandmother gave you and what time, you're supposed to leave in the morning." I sat up.

"How do you know?"

"It's my job, to know everything about my future."

"Your future?" His index finger went under my chin for him, to make me look in his eyes.

"I've never had a woman who's amazed me, as much as you do. You tell me no, and don't take my shit. You keep me calm and balanced. When I'm around you, all I want to do is protect you. Shorty, you got a nigga falling hard for you." I just stared at him.

"I'm in love with you Marco. There, I said it." I rolled over and he laughed.

"I'm in love with you too ma. I didn't wanna say it and scare you away."

"What are we going to do? I live so far and what if I wanna see you? How can we be together? I'm going to miss you?" I started rambling.

"Nothing, you said is a problem. I'll be there when you call and I'm going to miss you too. If I need to get a crib out there to be with you, I will." I nodded and laid my one arm across his waist and placed my head on his chest. He is everything I wanted in a man. I pray, he won't hurt me.

Cara

"Where's Rakia? Is she ok?" My mom asked, the next day when she got here. I shrugged my shoulders and told her, I hoped she got hit by a bus. She smacked the shit outta me.

"Ma."

"Don't ma, me. You know, she's a little different and you come for her all the time. What the fuck is wrong with you?" I sucked my teeth.

"Hey Cara! Are you feeling better?" I instantly got mad, seeing Rakia standing there with the *M* necklace Marco wears and a hickey on her neck. I saw the smile on my mom's face.

"Let me find out, my niece finally got her some." Rakia put her head down.

"Aunt Shanta, can we discuss this later? I only stopped by to check on Cara, before going back to school."

"Oh, we sure are." My mom went to take a call in the hallway.

"I don't know why you're so happy. If its Marco you slept with. He's nothing but a ho and.-"

"Why don't you like him Cara? Did he do something to you before last night?" I smirked. She was so gullible, I was about to break her fucking heart.

"That's what I was trying to tell you last night. Marco, called me in the bathroom with him and we had sex."

"You're lying." I could see her starting to shake.

"Why do you think he put his hands on me? I told him, what we did was wrong and should tell you. It's when he went into a rage." I sat up.

"He and I, have been sleeping together for over a year."

"I don't believe you."

"Rakia, I lost his baby last night." It was like the air, left her body as she fell against the wall.

"No! No! No! That's nottttt trueee." There goes the stuttering.

"I'm sorry Rak, but it is. He used you, to get back at me, for not wanting to be with him."

"I have to go." She said and bumped into my mom.

126

"Rakia, honey. What's wrong?"

"Nothing. I have to get to school."

"Rakia, you're not driving like this. You can barely stand. Sit." She pointed to a chair and Rakia listened but not for long. Once she took a look at me and saw me smiling, she ran out the room.

"What the fuck happened that fast?"

"She got a phone call and became upset. I don't know. Can I go home now?" She gave me an evil look but didn't question it.

The doctor came in an hour later and discharged me. I had some bruised ribs, a concussion and swelling in my neck and nose, otherwise, everything was good. I couldn't wait to take a hot bath.

I waited at the front entrance with the nurse, when my wheelchair started to move. I tried to turn around but my head was snapped back, to looking forward. The person, pushed me into some room and there was my worst nightmare, looking good as hell but scary at the same time. He disconnected the call he was on and looked at me.

"I'm gonna ask you one fucking time, what did you say to my girl."

"Your girl?"

"Yes, my fucking girl."

"You do know, she's retarded, right?" The backhand to my face, felt almost as bad, as the kick, to my ribs.

"Don't ever speak ill of her again." The blood dripped outta my nose and face quickly.

"Now, this is my last time asking. What did you say to my girl?"

"Nothing. She came to see me and ran out. I swear, I don't know."

"That's funny, you see. I told her not to come see you because you would say hurtful things to her, but she came anyway. You're her cousin and she wanted to make sure you were ok. I told her, you were poison and hateful but she didn't wanna believe it. Then, I get a call, from her hysterical crying about some shit you said to her." He stood next to me with a knife at my throat. I swallowed hard and asked why?

"We both know, when she gets like that, she shouldn't get behind the wheel of a car because it's not safe for her." I did know and it's the reason why, I made her so angry.

"You didn't care, said some shit to her and unfortunately; I couldn't get outta her what it was, you know why?" I shook my head no, as I felt the tip of the knife digging into the side my neck.

"BECAUSE SHE HIT A FUCKING TREE! MY GIRL IS LYING IN THE EMERGENCY ROOM, UNCONCIOUS FOR SOME FUCK SHIT YOU SAID." I could feel blood dripping down my neck as he, sliced it open. It felt like a doctor was cutting me open for surgery. He gave me an evil look.

"I'm not gonna kill you right now. Nah, I'm gonna wait and make you wonder, when I'm gonna take your life. And you better believe, I am." He lifted the knife and some guy handed him a towel.

"You better pray, she wakes up and if I find out, you said some fucked up shit to her, I'm going to kill you in front of your mother. Open the door." The guard did what he said and my mom came running in. She covered her mouth when she saw my neck and looked at Marco.

"Shanta, it's been a very long time." My mom nodded and said nothing.

"Let your daughter know, I'm not the one to be fucked with and if she so much as says, hello to my girl, I'll cut her fucking tongue out and make you eat it for dinner. Are we clear?" He pulled his sleeves on his shirt, down.

"Yes." We both said at the same time and watched him leave the room. My mom fell on the seat and gave me the deadliest stare ever.

"Cara, I don't know what you did to him or his girl but he's not someone to play with." I waved her off and asked if she could pass me some tissues out the box. Blood was drenching my shirt.

"His girl is Rakia."

"WHAT?"

"Exactly!" She started pacing back and forth.

"How do you know him?"

"I used to go with his father."

"Ma, really?"

"Yes, a few years ago, when you were a freshman, I met his dad and we fell in love. I never brought him around you because you were too grown and honestly, I was embarrassed. He used to give me money and still does, whenever I need it. Cara, he's the man, I wanted to marry but you broke us up with your lies."

"How did I break you up?"

"The day you were in my room, going through my stuff, you sent him a text message saying all these nasty things to him. He knew, I didn't speak that way and assumed, I was sleeping around. I tried to explain it wasn't me but he wouldn't even listen."

I remembered that day perfectly. I was in her room looking for something to wear to the first dance of the year. Her phone went off and it was a message from some guy named M.S. To be honest, I always thought my mom was a trick. Who knew she had been seeing the father of the man, I loved? Anyway, he sent her a message about dinner and I started being fresh. I don't know what happened, after I sent him an explicit ass message. I do know she was upset when I came home. It didn't cross my mind to ask what was wrong.

"What do you mean, he still gives you money?"

"He and I, have been seeing one another, privately. How do you think, I can afford the lifestyle we live?"

"I thought you were a ho." She smiled.

"And what are you?" My mouth dropped open. My mom knew I did my thing, shit, ever since Rakia went away to school, we've become a lot closer. Let's just say, we've done some crazy things together.

"What you better do, is make shit right with Rakia because I can't save you, if he comes for you. Hell, no one can." I ignored her and asked if she could take me to the ER. I had to get stitches because the cut had to be deep, for this much blood, to come out. I'll think of a reason on how this happened but I won't blame him, if he's right there.

Marco

Listening to Rakia, crying over some shit Cara told her, had me so mad, I wanted her cousins head on a platter. I couldn't even make out anything she said because of how hysterical she was. To make matters worse, I heard a loud noise and then she was quiet. I yelled her name but to no avail, did I get a response. I hopped in my car and drove in the direction of the hospital, hoping I'd find her truck and sure enough, there it sat, banged into a tree. The air bags deployed, which told me, the truck was ruined and she's hurt. I dialed 911 and waited. It was killing me, not to remove her from the truck and transport her to the hospital, myself. I knew, me doing it, could do more damage that way.

Once the EMT's arrived and put her in the ambulance, my ass got in with her. She was unconscious and bleeding from the head. There was a mark on her neck from the seatbelt and most likely the necklace, she wore. I gave it to her, to show off at school, along with the hickey. Everyone needed to know she was taken. The guy handed me the necklace when we got to the hospital.

I made a call to personnel, to see if one of the shorty's, I use to fuck with came in. She got on the phone and gave me the information requested. She had a nurse who owed her a favor, and put the request in for me, which is how, I got Cara. She told me where they would be and what room to go in and wait for her. The crazy part is, I had no idea, Shanta was her mom. I thought, I saw her on Thanksgiving but wasn't sure.

I met her mom through my dad, quite a few times. She was cool as hell and even tried to get me with her daughter. Once she told me her age, I was good. Shanta was in love with my pops but he left her alone; saying she text him some shit and it made him think she was cheating. He asked me to check into it and come to find out she wasn't. Evidently, the daughter, who turned out to be Cara, was being grown and sent the messages.

Now, I'm standing here waiting for the doctor to come tell me something. Shanta, pushed Cara in with tissues on her neck and blood all over her clothes. I smirked and dared her to pull the snitching shit, she did yesterday. The bitch is from the streets and knows the code. I should kill her for that but again, I'm trying my hardest not to hurt Rak. She tries to see the good in everyone and it would devastate her. Something tells me Cara, knows it and that's why she does the shit but I got something for her ass, next time.

"Mr. Santiago." The doctor came over in my direction.

"Yes." He extended his hand for me to shake.

"Ms. Winters is.-"

"Hold up. He's not a family member." Cara yelled and if I could kill her with my eyes, she'd be dead.

"Shut the fuck up before the person who did that to you, comes back and does worse."

"I doubt he'll do anything here." She smirked.

"Then you don't know him very well." She shut right up, when my guard walked over to her.

"Like I was saying." The doctor continued.

"Ms. Winters, suffered a concussion, a chest contusion; most likely from the steering wheel hitting her chest and she has a few stitches above her forehead. Besides all that, she's

135

fine. I ran a MRI and Cat Scan but I would like her to stay overnight for observation." He shook my hand and told me they put her in a room and the exact floor she was on. I stopped at the gift shop and picked up a few balloons, flowers and a teddy bear.

She was asleep when I walked in, so I sat everything on the table. There were monitors on her chest, a blood pressure cuff and an IV, in her arm. She looked so peaceful lying there. I placed a soft kiss on her lips and slid in bed beside her. I must've dosed off because my guard had to wake me up, to say some old woman was outside tryna get in.

"It's ok." I looked down and Rak was smiling at me.

"You ok?"

"I have a headache and need the bathroom." I pushed the button for the nurse. She came in and helped her out the bed, to do what she needed.

"Who are you?" The old woman asked.

"Marco Santiago, ma'am." I extended my hand and she pulled me in for a hug.

"I don't know you but I want to thank you, for finding her. She may not be here, if it weren't for you."

"The accident wasn't that bad but I understand your concern."

"It may not have looked that way to you but Rakia, should've never been driving. She gets so upset, it's hard for her to calm down."

"I agree. Trust me, I'm gonna handle that, even if I have to drive her everywhere, myself."

"Listen." She glanced over at the bathroom.

"I know my granddaughter Cara, had something to do with this."

"Oh, she did."

"Do me a favor and keep Rakia away from her. Cara hates her and always has."

"Why?"

"I don't have time to explain right now but she wants to see Rakia hurt, or even dead."

"I'm gonna do my best to keep her away but Rakia loves her. It's gonna be hard. Shit, I told her not to come see her but she had to make sure Cara was ok."

"Rakia's heart is pure. No matter, how many times you hurt her, she'll still be your friend. She's never been one to hold grudges. As far as men, she's never had one, so please handle her with care."

"No doubt."

"Grandma, this is Marco and Marco, this is my grandmother." She introduced us, but we already got acquainted.

"Can I go home? I have school in the morning and.-"

"Don't worry about school."

"Marco, I'm not dropping out to be with you."

"I wasn't gonna say that but damn. You don't really love me."

"I didn't mean it like that. I'm just saying, I worked very hard to get in."

"I'm just fucking with you. I was gonna say, we'll call the school tomorrow and explain what happened. You have proof, you were in an accident and had to stay overnight. They'll most likely give you the rest of the week off, to rest."

"You think so. I mean, I'm all caught up on work in those classes and even did extra credit stuff. They won't fail me, right?" I had to hug her. I loved this woman and her nervousness, always did something to me.

"They better not fail you, or they'll be dealing with me."

"Oh grandma. I forgot, Marco is my boyfriend."

"Boyfriend." I questioned and gave her the side eye.

"My man. I'm sorry." She kissed my lips and her grandmother smiled.

"Why is everyone so cheerful in here?" Cara came in with her mom and my eyes probably had slits in them. She had a huge bandage on her neck. Angela and Tech, walked in behind them and he must've already knew what was up because he asked me to come in the hallway.

"I'll be right outside the door." Cara rolled her eyes.

"Ok baby." I kissed her lips and dared this dumb bitch to open her mouth. Tech grabbed me out the room. I made sure

139

to stand where I could see Rak and possibly hear what the fuck Cara spit out her mouth.

"Whoever those niggas were, plan on returning." I knew exactly who he referred to. When you knock a motherfucker out, of course, they'll retaliate.

"Where did they come from?" I asked because everyone knew exactly who we were and never even tried, what this nigga did.

"They're definitely from outta town. I'm not sure they came to cop from you but they're damn sure here, for something or someone."

"We need to get our computer guy a copy of the video and have him do facial recognition on them. I wanna know who their family is and their addresses. If he wants to try some shit, then we have no choice but to show him, how we get down."

"That's exactly, why you in charge because I wanted to say, let's just kill them now."

"We need to calculate our moves bro. We may have law enforcement on our side but the less unnecessary drama, the better. And bro, you're in charge too. You know, I hate when you say shit like that." I punched him in the chest. Tech may have started working later than I did, but he was still my equal. He knew, how much I hated him saying it too. The nigga loved to get under my skin.

"Just go Cara." We heard and I went inside the room to find Rak crying.

"What the fuck, yo?"

"Nothing, Marco."

"Fuck that bitch, Rak. Tell him." Ang, shouted.

"Tell me what?" She wouldn't say anything and I saw Shanta and the grandmother, shaking their head.

"Your buddy Cara here, told Rakia, you and her have been an item and she lost your baby."

"WHAT?" I was so fucking mad.

"Bitch, we never fucked. Yo, I'm done with this ho." I pulled my gun out and put it to her head. I was about to pull the trigger and didn't give a fuck about anyone calling the cops. I own them motherfuckers.

"Marco, please don't." I felt Rakia's arms wrapped around my waist. My finger was itching.

"Marco." She cried out again and I put my hand down and hit the bitch so hard, she fell out the wheelchair. Shanta jumped up screaming because this bitch started bleeding on her head but a nigga was over her shit. I bent down and whispered in her ear.

"If you ever in your fucking life, lie to my girl again, I swear on everything, no one will be able to stop me from pulling the motherfucking trigger."

"Your girl. Was she your girl the other day when you and Bobbi came out the mall, from shopping together? Huh?" Rakia moved her hands away. I forgot all about seeing this dumb bitch there.

"Was she your girl, when you kissed her in the parking lot, to let me know, you were taken? You getting mad at me, when you hiding a lot of secrets."

"Marco, I know we weren't together yet but you told me, the Bobbi chick was no longer in your life. Is what Cara

142

saying true? Were you kissing her in the parking lot?" Shanta was helping her in the chair.

"Yea, Marco. Tell her the truth. Tell her about New York, too."

"You tryna die, today?" I heard Tech ask, but couldn't pay attention right now because the tears cascading down Rakia's face, were distracting me.

"Rakia, you told me on Thanksgiving, you couldn't give me what I wanted. You told me to leave you alone."

"And you told me, you're not going to believe, I didn't want you the same way."

"It doesn't mean, I was gonna sit around twiddling my thumbs. When you were ready, I would drop everyone."

"You said, you weren't giving up. Did you give up on me? Marco, I gave you all of me. How could you?" She looked at Shanta wheeling Cara out.

"Is that what you were trying to tell me Cara?"

"About New York, yup. I didn't know about him and Bobbi, until I saw them at the mall. But I'm the bad guy, when all I was doing, is looking out for you. Rakia, you chose to believe him over your own family and look where it got you."

Her mom wheeled her out.

"Rak. Let me talk to you, privately." She looked at me with an evil glare. I didn't even know she got angry. Shit, she always had a smile on her face.

"I don't have anything else to say to you. It's over. Please leave."

"Nah."

"JUST GO MARCO. YOU CAN'T FIX THIS." She shouted and fell back on the bed, crying. Angela ran over to cradle her. I sat there staring at how, I broke her just that quick. I know how fragile she is and instead of being truthful about everything, it blew up on my face. Yea, I was still fucking Bobbi and a few other bitches but it was before, she and I, had sex or made it official.

Tech sat in the chair waiting for Angela and Rakia's grandmother, sat there with a few tears coming down her face. I literally just told her, I'd protect Rakia and here I fucked up. There's no doubt in my mind, Cara did this for her own reasons.

I watched her get in the bed, under the covers and didn't miss her turning the other way, so she didn't have to face me. I stood up and walked over to her. I ran my hand down her face and kissed her forehead. I messed up and blame myself, for not mentioning it but I stand by my decision, not too. She wasn't my girl and we had no verbal contract, stating we couldn't mess with anyone else. I swear, once she gave herself to me, that was it though. I cut everyone off; including Bobbi. I guess, it didn't matter now.

Angela

I felt so bad for Rakia. She was so excited this morning when she called, to tell me about their night. The way she spoke of how he catered to her all night and before she left, made me smile. She's gone through so much in her life and deserved to feel true love. However, Cara made sure to throw a monkey wrench in their quick relationship. The smirk on her face pissed me off but I couldn't do shit, with a baby in my stomach and Tech's, at that. He would kill me if anything happened. I'll hold off on beating her ass but the ass whooping, is waiting.

After Marco left, I told Tech, to go too. He wasn't too happy and I didn't care. He did go grab both of us, something to eat and brought it back. I still wasn't really speaking to him either, over the phone call. I should talk about it; however, my body doesn't need any stress, right now. That too, will be addressed, when I drop this load.

"He wasn't supposed to cheat." Rakia cried. Her grandmother left ten minutes ago, so it was only the two of us. I wasn't about to sugar coat anything to appease her.

"Rakia, He didn't cheat on you." She sat up.

"But he.-"

"He what? Continued getting his dick wet because you weren't giving him any? Or he shouldn't take her shopping or spend time with her, even though you told him not to wait for you and you didn't wanna be with him! Or that, maybe he did do something with Cara, but it was before your time?"

"Yea, but he should've told me before we, you know." I handed her a tissue for her nose.

"Told you, for what?" She looked at me.

"What he does, is his business, Rakia. Why would he openly tell you, he fucked or is fucking other people? Think about it. You wouldn't commit to him, so he kept it moving. Now you're crying over some bullshit Cara told you, that happened before you slept with him and became his girl. You have to stop letting her get in the middle of you two."

"You're right."

"Have you told him about, Zaire?"

"Well no but.-" Zaire was this guy, she met at school. He was a distraction from her crush with Marco. He was a handsome guy, from what she told me and they spent a lot of time together. She never allowed him to touch her and the kiss they shared, he basically stole because she turned around and he caught her. I told her to go ahead and give the man some but she claimed not to be feeling him like that.

"But what?"

"We didn't do anything. I mean, he kissed me but I pulled away."

"It doesn't matter, Rak. You have someone at school and you're mad at him, for doing the exact same thing you did."

"Maybe, I should call him." She picked the phone up. It rang and he didn't answer. The damn stalker, called back two more times, back to back. I had to snatch the phone from her. She kept saying he probably didn't hear it. I swear, she was gullible as fuck, when it came to men.

"Look. He's probably upset, so we'll try him tomorrow."

"No. I wanna see him." She started taking the monitors off her body and putting clothes on. No matter, what I said, she wanted to see him so I had the doctor come in. He advised her not to leave but couldn't hold her against her will. He handed her the discharge papers and I called an UBER to pick us up. Her truck was totaled and I didn't drive. Tech kept trying to buy me a car but I refused. My ass walked everywhere so cabs were nothing to me. She had the driver take us to the club first because she didn't want to take the long drive to his house.

"Thank you." We got out at the club and asked the Uber driver to wait, just in case he wasn't there.

"There's his truck." It was parked on the side but you could still see it.

"He probably needed a drink." She started walking and for some reason, I knew this would end bad. The truck was moving and I'm not talking about pulling off.

"Marco. Baby, are you?-" She opened the door and froze. He had some chick bent over his back seat, naked and it wasn't Bobbi. Why didn't he lock the damn door? Shit, I had to turn my head because I didn't wanna see no other man's dick. He had all his clothes on but I still wasn't taking any chances.

"Rak, what are you doing out the hospital?" She didn't respond. I turned around and grabbed her hand. It was like she couldn't move.

"Let's go."

"I… I… I… don't know what to say Ang. He told me, he'd never cheat and I was mad, at what Cara said but why did he run to another woman? I must not have been good enough for him. Ang, I wanna go home."

"RAKIA!" He shouted and came running behind us.

"Really, Marco?" I heard the woman say.

"Rakia, look. I'm sorry ma."

"Why Marco?"

"I was drinking because you told me to leave and she pulled me out here and FUCK! Ma, I'm so sorry."

"Did you know you were having sex with her?"

"Huh?"

"You said, you were drinking." She stood in front of him.

"Does she look like me?"

"RAK."

"DOES SHE?" She shouted, shocking both of us. He ran his hand down his face. People were coming in and out the club and some were being nosy.

"Nah, ma. She don't."

"EXACTLY! Which means, your dick should've never been in her." He didn't say anything.

"You're no good for me, Marco."

"What?" She tried to get in the Uber.

"GET OFF ME." She snatched away and his entire facial expression changed.

"Calm the fuck down Rak."

"Calm down, Marco. You expect me to be calm, after I catch you fucking some woman in your truck? You want me to be calm, after you said, you'd never cheat?"

"Once again, I didn't cheat. You told me it was over and to leave you alone. Look, I don't need motherfuckers in my business. If you wanna discuss this elsewhere, let's go."

"This is my fault Ang. I should've never tried to love a man like him? Right? He's too mature and I haven't grown up yet. I can't handle a man like him. What was I thinking? I'm so stupid." She rambled on and I could see his demeanor change from angry to sad. I could tell he loved her but he really fucked up.

"Yo, is she crazy or something?" I heard someone ask and outta nowhere, Marco knocked him out. I heard his head hit the pavement and jumped back.

"Anybody else, got something to say?" Everyone put their hands up. I called Tech on the phone and he didn't answer but his car was here. I asked the Uber driver to pull up the street and not to leave. I wanted him to think she left but I had to get Tech out here, to calm him down. His security was having a hard time.

I walked in the club and couldn't find him, anywhere. I made my way up the steps and to his office. Now, with Marco outside fucking some bitch, all I could think was, if I opened

this door and he's fucking, I don't know what, I'd do. I decided

to leave because I'm not sure, I could handle it. However, the

door opened and some chick walked out, wiping her mouth.

She looked me up and down and yelled for Tech. He came to

the door and stopped short, when he saw me.

"Today, must be, cheat on your women day."

"Ang, what you doing here?" I threw my head back

laughing.

"I come to find you because your boy out there bugging

and the first thing you ask is, what am I doing here? I should

expect this, being your boy just got caught, doing the exact

same thing."

"Ang, it's not what you think."

"Tech, arc you serious right now?" The chick asked. I

didn't even know she was still standing there.

"Who are you?"

"Oh, I'm the bitch who'll, suck and fuck your man,

when you won't." I nodded.

"This is what you've become Tech? You don't get no pussy at home, so you run to the club and fuck one of you stripper employees?"

"I didn't fuck her Ang."

"Oh no. Well your zipper is down and she has white shit in the crease of her mouth, so if you didn't fuck, I'm gonna assume, she sucked you off." He leaned his head back on the wall and she smirked.

"Crazy, right?" I said and punched her in the face. She hit the wall and I hooked off again, until Tech pulled me off.

"Fuck you nigga. Stay the hell away from me." I smacked the hell outta him and ran down the steps. I had to catch myself because I almost fell.

"ANGELA!" He shouted and I hauled ass, out the club. Marco, was gone by now and I saw the lights from the Uber driver and ran as fast, as I could. I hopped in the car and asked the guy to pull off. I saw Tech tryna chase it.

"What happened Ang?" I laid my head back and asked the driver to take us to the hospital. My stomach was in knots and I was cramping.

"He cheated, sis."

"NO!" I wiped my eyes.

"Yup and I'm ok, believe it or not."

"How can you say that? You're upset and crying."

"I knew Rak."

"Huh?"

"The phone call from the other night, was probably her. I prepared myself for it, to come out. The reason, I'm upset and crying is because he could've at least waited until I gave birth. I would've handled it better. Its ok though. We're both young and can move on." I grabbed her hand and she kept telling me to try and relax. My phone started ringing and I tossed it out the window.

"What are we gonna do, Ang?" She was sitting in the chair at the hospital.

"Keep it pushing? You're stronger than you think Rak. We'll get through this together." She stood up and grabbed my hand.

"I hope so."

****

"He's gonna come here." Rakia said when she dropped me off at school.

Since her truck was gone, we rented one to return to school. Both of us, called the Dean of our schools and made up a story about being stalked by some man in our town. It took some convincing, but we had proof from being in the hospital, so it worked out fine.

She got a new dorm, totally opposite from her old one and so did I. We were both excused from our classes for two weeks and had to get the assignments from the teacher's email. I didn't think we could pull off a disappearance on those niggas but we did. I hope we stay hidden.

Tech

FUCK! FUCK! FUCK! I shouted out, to no one. I put my hands-on top of my head and walked back towards the club. A few people, spoke on my way in and others were leaving. I walked in and towards my office, when Shana, the stripper who came out my office, stood in front of me. I looked her up and down and scoffed up a laugh. Shorty, was bad and the pussy is decent but it wasn't worth losing my girl over. The crazy part is, I didn't fuck her.

Ang, asked me to leave the hospital so her and Rak, could talk alone. I didn't want to because over these last few days of her being home for Thanksgiving, something's been off. Every time I ask her, she refuses to mention it. Never mind the fact, we haven't had sex, except the first night she got here. I'm not worried about her being with someone else, because my kid is in her stomach. It doesn't excuse the cold shoulder she's been given me.

Anyway, I got here and Marco was in VIP alone. I could tell he wanted to strangle, well murder Cara, for revealing those lies. The only reason he didn't is because of the hurt it would instill on Rak. We all know how forgiven she is and he knew, she'd forgive her cousin. About an hour after getting there, both of us were tipsy as hell, from all the Hennessy we drank. Some chick came and asked to speak to him outside, and I took my ass in my office. Little did I know, Shana was right behind me. I asked what she wanted and of course, she was complaining because I had someone.

I sat down and she came over to my desk. I watched her remove her clothes and yea, my dick got hard. I shook my head, stood up and handed her the clothes. She stuck her hands in my jeans, pulled my dick out and like any man, I failed victim to her giving me head. After she swallowed my kids, I went in the bathroom and told her to get out. I stared at myself in the mirror and knew I'd have to come clean to Ang. I'm not into keeping secrets. It didn't take me long to reveal it because when I was leaving, she stood outside the door with hurt written all over her face. Shana started talking shit and got her ass beat.

Now, she standing here talking about getting Ang back. I told her if she laid one hand on her, she'd come up missing. How these bitches talk shit and once they get their ass beat, wanna make threats. Take the ass whooping and keep it moving. I had security let her out the club and told her she was suspended for a week, for causing drama in my club. She knew I didn't play that and I'm not about to start.

I drove to Ang's school, the following day and the RA, or whoever he was, said he had to pack up her things because she dropped outta school. I didn't believe it and had him take me to her room. Sure enough, her room was cleaned out. I asked where did the things go and he gave me an address, which was to her parents' house. I hopped in the car and sped there.

****

"You must've cheated on her." Her fake ass mother said, when she opened the door.

"Where is she?"

159

"I don't know. My husband got a call saying she was ok and didn't wanna be found. He asked over and over, what happened and she refused to tell him. I can only assume you fucked up, if you're here and don't know her whereabouts."

"Fuck outta here yo." I waved her off and went to leave.

"I hope she keeps my grandson away from you."

"Grandson. You don't even like her." I was shocked to hear her say grandson. Ang, never told me the sex of the baby.

"Is that what you think? Let me tell you something, young man." She walked up on me by my car.

"That woman was raised by me, even after the vial things, her real mother and father did to me."

"Huh?"

"Exactly. You probably heard I was mean to her but it wasn't what you think. If she got smart, you damn right, I popped her in the mouth. If she was failing in school, I was in her ass. I'm the one who helped her pick the college she's in. I was the one, who helped her when she first got her period, her first heartbreak and all the other first things, she went though. So, before you judge me off of false stories, look into my

160

world and see what I went through, raising another woman's child by a man, I believed could do no wrong." She left me standing there looking crazy. Ang, never really spoke about the family issues but it's obvious other shit went on. I guess, I'll never know, because she won't even speak to me.

"Ang, I know you see me calling. I'm sorry bae. Please answer the phone and tell me you're ok." I left her another message, like I've been doing everyday since she left. I hope one of these days, she'll pick up.

****

"Yo." I answered my phone without looking. I was on my way to meet Marco. We found out who the guys were that came to the club.

"I miss you." Ang said and I could hear her sniffling in the phone. I pulled my truck over.

"Ang, it's been three months. Where are you?"

"Home."

"Home? How long have you been in town?"

"I never went back to school after Christmas break."

"I thought you dropped out and I came by on Christmas."

"I know. My dad was against sending you away but he did it for me."

"You good. Is my son, ok?"

"Yea and how did you know?"

"Your mom told me." She sucked her teeth.

"Are you busy Tech?"

"I'm about to have a meeting with Marco. What you need?"

"I just wanted to talk. I need to know why, I wasn't enough."

"Ang, I promise, that wasn't it. Let me go to this meeting and I'll hit you up as soon as I leave. Is this your new number?" I asked because she changed it.

"Yea."

"Bet. Give me an hour." She hung up as I pulled back onto the road.

The entire ride over to meet Marco, all I thought about was getting her back. I know, for a fact, she's gonna give me a hard time but she's worth the begging and pleading. Ang, isn't any woman who wasn't about shit. She was a few years younger than me, however, her mentality was more mature than other women, my age and older. She cooked, cleaned, gave me some of the best sex, I ever had and she had my heart. It was up to me, to make sure she didn't disappear again and hopefully, whatever I come up with, will help.

"What's up?" I walked in the meeting spot and it was only a few of us here. Marco and I, didn't trust anyone. Therefore, if it was a meeting, it would only be, with a handful.

"Ok, so the guys who came trying to start some beef, are from Connecticut. I'm not sure why they're here, or even the reason to try us in the club. I do know, they're well aware of who we are, and at this very moment, putting together a team to get at us."

"What you wanna us to do?" Doc asked.

"From here on out, keep a watchful eye on who works under you. One or some of them, could be working with them or handing out information."

"How much do they know?"

"Right now, nothing, which means, no one in this room is running their mouth. You were each chosen to handle shit and so far, you've done that, without slip-ups. Go head Marco." I handed the floor to him.

"Due to your loyalty and silence, you have all been rewarded with a hefty check inside these envelopes." They all smiled.

Marco, never gave them anything less than 75k for bonuses. Even though he was the plug, he still had a team under him, making more money. The people who copped from him, didn't live around us, therefore, it was no reason to have a sit down with them because they knew nothing. Whoever, these people are, wanted beef with us and of course, if we need help, one of us would reach out but it's not likely. The ones we had were pretty thorough and with every organization, there's always a hater.

"I did put bonuses in there for your workers. However, I want you to sit each one down and make sure, they're well aware of what happens to snitches and their families. Pay attention, to their facial expressions and body movements. A nervous nigga, will give himself away, without saying a word. But never underestimate, the ones who don't either."

"Well, how would we know?"

"Good question. As the leader; you know your team and should be able to sniff out the rat. The changes will show eventually and when it does, I want him brought straight to me and Tech. Do not and I repeat, do not try and handle anything on your own. If the person figures out you know, he'll run and I would hate for you to get caught up and no one have your back because you were being tough." They all nodded. Marco and I, discussed other things with them, such as, distribution and pickups before we left.

Afterwards, I hit Ang up and had her meet me at her favorite place, which has been Outback Steakhouse, since the pregnancy. Once she told me ok, I headed straight there. A nigga was hungry and anxious to see my girl. Say what you want but she will be mine again.

Angela

I know people are gonna think, I'm weak for contacting Tech. However, find me a woman who's had a man and he never cheated. They can try and say not their man but shit, we know it's not the truth. In this day and age, cheating comes in so many forms, that sexual intercourse, isn't the only one. I'm talking about cheating emotionally, mentally, sexting, the DM's, inboxes and even flirting, are considered not being faithful. All these things, can be done with the one person you love but once you start entertaining another woman or man, its cheating.

Anyway, I stayed away for a few months to get my head on straight and to hear if, he actually continued messing with anyone else. Word on the street was, he didn't have a girl and no one seen him out with anyone. It's not to say it isn't happening but he wasn't out in the open. I couldn't really say much if he were but it would make it a lot harde, to even be around him.

Before Christmas break, I applied for online classes at NYU. There was no way, I'd be able to finish the entire next semester on campus and I didn't wanna lose credit or have to start over. Online was easier but I did miss the campus life. Going back and forth to class, meeting different people and living in a dorm, is the best. I had my own privacy and could have anyone there, at any time. Unfortunately, the only person, I wanted was in New Jersey and under the assumption, I was missing. I was but only to him. Now, I'm standing in the door at my favorite place, staring at how good he looked.

His dreads were freshly done, his tattoos were peeking under his t-shirt and his light brown eyes, were focusing on the menu. Tech, was a very handsome man and I hated and loved it. Women threw themselves at him and he didn't entertain them. However, if the stripper chick was able to get him, he must be. I swear, he made my heart skip a beat, every time we were together and today, was no different. Making my way over to him, I felt someone staring but when I looked, it seemed like everyone in there, were engaged in their own conversation.

"Hello." He turned around and the smile that graced his face, put one on mine.

"My son is getting big." He stood and rubbed on my stomach.

"Yea, the doctor said, he's already at four pounds and I still have two more months to go."

"Sit." He pulled the chair out for me and leaned down to kiss my lips. I allowed it and we didn't stop until the waitress, cleared her throat to take our order. We gave her our choices and she walked away but not without licking her lips at him. Of course, its disrespectful but he never took his eyes off me, so I let it go.

"How have you been?" I shrugged my shoulders.

"Ang, I'm sorry. It's no excuse for allowing her to touch me and hurt you, the way I did."

"How long were you cheating with her?"

"That is the only time. I've never cheated, since we've been together."

"Then why?"

"I don't even know. You came home for Thanksgiving, gave me the cold shoulder, wouldn't have sex with me and answered me with one word. I had no idea what was up and then, you asked me to leave the hospital. When I went to the club, Marco and I, drank mad Hennessey and he walked out to speak with someone. I went up to my office and Shana, was right behind me. She began stripping, I tossed her clothes at her and told her to get dressed. Unfortunately, with the liquor in my system, I didn't fight her, when she reached in my jeans, to suck me off. I swear, on my unborn son Ang, I kicked her out right after. No sex took place and I was coming home to tell you. I'm not a secret keeping nigga." I nodded.

He always said, he'd tell me the truth, whether it would hurt me or not, so when he said, he planned on telling me, I believed him. It probably wouldn't have hurt as much, hearing it and not seeing them afterwards. What am I saying, of course, it still would've hurt?

"The reason, I gave you the cold shoulder is because the night I came home, a woman called and hung up twice. Then she cursed me out." He gave me a crazy look.

"Did you call her back? Better yet, why didn't you tell me?" I shrugged my shoulders.

"Ang, I'm not saying its why I let her go down on me, because it wasn't. I was drunk but you should've said something and let me handle it. Instead, you shut down and left me hanging."

"I'm sorry and you're right, I should've.-" The waitress came and placed our meals in front of us.

"No disrespect but you are fine."

"Bitch, are you crazy? You see my woman sitting here and you tryna fuck. Beat it." Her mouth flew open. She rolled her eyes and walked away. I smiled at him, referencing me as his woman.

"Well, I'm glad our food came out before you flipped."

"I saw her the first time but you're right. I had to wait for her to bring it out, so she wouldn't spit in it. I would say let's leave but I know you're hungry and really wanted to eat here."

"Thanks, I guess." I picked my fork and knife up, to cut my steak. I absolutely loved their blooming onion but my favorite, is their steak and potatoes.

"Mmmm, its so good." I opened my eyes and he was staring at me.

"What's wrong?"

"A nigga, missed the hell outta you." I could feel my face turning red.

"Ummm."

"Don't say anything. I'm gonna do everything I can, to get you back." He reached over and used his thumb to wipe the lone tear that fell down my face.

"Well, isn't this cute?" I looked up and my anger got the best of me. I spit the mashed potatoes in her face. Tech, jumped out his seat and stood in front of me.

"Get the fuck on, Shana."

"Tech, this how you do me, after all we've been through?"

"All we been though? Bitch, we use to fuck, you sucked my dick and that's it. Don't come over here with no bullshit, knowing it ain't even like that." I learned two things tonight. One… he didn't care, I spit in her face and defended me, regardless. And two… this bitch is going to be a problem, going forward.

"Tech, how you let her spit in my face?"

"You came over here to start shit and got what you got. Be out Shana, or its gonna be a problem."

"I'm gonna get.-" He never let her finish and held her up by the neck.

"Don't ever threaten her again. I'll fucking kill you." She didn't say anything. He tossed her on the ground, grabbed my hand and threw money on the table.

"You ok?" He checked me over in the parking lot and had me get in the car with him.

"Where are you going?"

"I'm taking you to my house, so we can finish talking. If you wanna go home, after, I'll take you."

The drive over, we kept stealing glances at one another. I felt like a big ass teenager, going to be with my crush for the first time. He would smile, then I would and he'd kiss my hand.

172

It was like old times with us. I ended up falling asleep on the way there. He opened the car door for me and I popped my eyes open. He helped me out and closed the front door, when we stepped inside.

"You redecorated?" I asked, looking in the house. It used to be all red. Now, its black and silver, which are my favorite colors.

"I did it for you."

"Tech."

"Come here." He grabbed my hand and led me upstairs.

"Oh my God!" I covered my mouth and walked in the room.

There was a black crib, with a silver comforter set. The walls were silver with a splash of black in it. The rocking chair was black and so was the footstool in front of it. There was a changing table, basinet, and a stroller set inside, with all types of diapers, wipes and other things. The closet was full of onesies and some baby Jordan's, of course. The wall had Antoine, written on it, in those letters you get from the baby store and there were small animals painted on the wall. I turned around and he had a huge smile on his face.

"You did all this by yourself and what if we were having a girl?"

"Yes, I did and your mom told me, it was a boy but if we were." He grabbed my hand and led me in another room. I shook my head because this room was decorated for a baby girl.

"You were gone but you and my child, have always been on my mind. I knew, you'd come back to at least, deliver and I wanted to show you, I wasn't no deadbeat."

"I would've never thought that." I left the room and went to see the other changes he made. It was like a brand-new house.

"Tell me what to do, in order, to get you home." I stood there allowing him to feel me up.

"You have to figure it out because I don't even know."

"Sex, doesn't make everything go away but I know you need me, as much as, I need you." He whispered behind me and removed my clothes. Luckily, I showered before leaving the house.

"Be careful, ma." I lifted my leg on his shoulder, while still standing. He was nervous about me falling.

"Ssssssss. It feels good." I came instantly and he made sure to catch anything leaving my body.

"Oh gawddddd." I shouted, after feeling his fingers inside my hole. I couldn't hold out any longer and gave him some more, of what he desperately wanted.

"Taste good, as always. Can I make love to you?" I moved on the bed and waited for him to enter and when he did, I screamed out.

"Shit, you ok?"

"Yea. It's been a while and I have to get used to you again. Don't stop." He started slow and then, went at his usual pace.

"Don't cry, Ang. You fucking me up." He kissed my tears away and continued making love to me. I promise, I came at least six times.

"You don't have to, Ang." I moved down his body, the best I could with this big ass stomach and found, what I was looking for.

"Tell me, if it's not what you want."

"I'll always want, whatever you offer." He sat on his elbows, to watch me. I opened my mouth and swallowed as much, as I could.

"Fuck, Ang." His hand went to my hair and he guided me up and down, the way he wanted.

"I love you so fucking much, Ang. Come home. Ahhhh." He moaned and came in my mouth.

"I am home, Tech. You have to figure out a way, to keep me here." I went in the bathroom to shower and he was right behind me.

****

"Do you Angela Powers, take Antoine Miller, to be your lawfully wedded husband. To have and to hold, til death do you part?" Yes, he dragged me down to the courthouse, as a way to show me, he meant everything he said about keeping me in his life.

176

"I do." My father cleared his throat and Marco, started laughing. My dad, loved Tech but he also wanted me to wait a few years to get married.

"And Antoine Miller."

"I do, I do. Hurry up, so I can kiss my bride." Now, I had to laugh. He was a fool.

"Um, ok." The reverend said and hurried up to finish. Once he called us husband and wife, Tech put both hands on my face and kissed me so passionate, I still had my eyes closed, when he finished.

"Alright damn, Ang. You can open your eyes now with your dramatic ass." I stuck my finger up at Marco.

"Thanks for becoming my wife. I promise, not to hurt you again." I nodded and he took my hand in his.

"Nigga, aren't you supposed to carry her out or something?" Marco, had jokes for days.

"Soon as we get on our honeymoon; I'ma carry that ass, all over my face, and then we're gonna.-"

"Yo, what the fuck? I don't wanna hear nothing, you two perverts do." I walked over to Marco and kissed his cheek, after I pinched both of them. He sucked his teeth and told me, to stay away from him. I asked why and he said, because I came back without Rak. I couldn't stop laughing. He was such a brat.

"You said, to figure out something to keep you. Are you happy?" Tech asked on our way to the airport. He booked us tickets to Italy. I've always wanted to go there to shop and see the sites. I was so excited, he had to make me stop jumping up and down.

"Very. Thank you."

"I'll do anything for you. Don't ever forget that." He pecked my lips and I laid my head on his shoulders.

The wedding we had, was extra small but as long as, he was the one waiting on me at the altar; I didn't need anyone else. I'm sure Rakia, is going to kill me for not telling her and she missed it. Hopefully, he put the bitch Shana, in check because I'm not about to be fighting over my husband. Its sounds crazy calling him that, but I love it.

I looked down at my gigantic ring, he picked out before I came back. Evidently, he planned on proposing on

Christmas but he didn't see me. Anyway, these bitches better

recognize, I'm the fucking wife. Ain't no more sharing my

man.

I hope this is my happily ever after because Lord knows,

I can use one.

Rakia

"Come on Rak. We've known one another for a while now." Zaire said and tried to place his hand under my shirt, again.

"I'm on my period." He sucked his teeth. I wasn't lying about bleeding, it's just that, it was over two days ago. Don't get me wrong, this man is fine as hell but I wasn't ready to have sex with anyone.

After Marco and I, had that wonderful night and early morning, I went to see my cousin in the hospital and she gave me the disturbing news, of losing his child. I shouldn't have been driving but I was distraught and needed to see Marco, for him to tell me it was a lie. I ended up crashing and totaling my truck. Long story short, the truth came out later, or did it. He said she was lying, she claimed it was the truth and I had no clue, who to believe.

My heart was beating for Marco and all I wanted to do, was be with him, regardless; of what Cara told me. I left the hospital in search for him. The joke was on me, when I opened the door to his truck and caught him fucking the hell outta some chick. I froze, and it wasn't to keep watching but more because my ass, was in shock. How could he say, he was in love with me and have sex with another woman, in the same twenty-four hours?

Anyway, I went back to school and after a month or so, I was having the worst cramps ever and my period wasn't here. I never paid any attention to the fact, of us not using condoms or that, I hadn't menstruated. I ran to the store to buy a test and was indeed notified, of my pregnancy. I called his phone one night and some chick answered and told me to never call again. Of course, I did anyway but it continuously went to voicemail. I told Angela how I tried to reach him, just to talk and what the chick said. I never told her about the pregnancy because he should've been the first one informed. She said, whoever the chick was, must've blocked me. I didn't feel like, I should chase him, and he should do better about watching who he leaves his phone around.

Two weeks later, I went to the clinic, had the procedure done and cried every night. I made an attempt to call him again and it went straight to voicemail. I thought about asking Angela to have Tech, tell him to call me but I was over everything. It's obvious, he moved on, so it's time to move on, which is where Zaire, comes in.

Zaire, goes to school here and he's in his second year of the law program. He is very smart and handsome. A lot, of the women on campus wanted him, yet, he was always under me. Zaire, put me in the mind frame of, a younger Allen Iverson, who played for Phila, some years back. I only know who he was because of the three on three, Ice-Cube had in California. Baller Alert posted mad photos of the event.

He and I, have been seeing each other, since before Thanksgiving. At first, he would flirt with me and stole a kiss. I never said anything because in my eyes, it was nothing. When I came home for the holiday and slept with Marco, I had plans on leaving him alone. Unfortunately, things didn't work out and the two of us, been together ever since.

"Fine. I'll see you later then." He stood up and started to grab his things.

"You're mad because I won't have sex with you?" I had my arms folded across my chest.

"See it the way you want. I'm not about to keep playing games with you." He pushed past me and it felt like, he was gonna knock my shoulder off.

"HEY! That wasn't nice." He laughed.

"And you being a dick tease, isn't either."

"What's a dick tease?"

"Someone who, continues to make you think you're gonna fuck and then don't." I covered my mouth and he slammed the door.

I locked the door and grabbed my things to go in my room and start on this paper. My teacher said it's not due for another month but I like to get things over with, just in case, I don't feel like doing it later.

I sat in front of my computer for hours. Unfortunately, my focus was gone because of the shit, Zaire said. Was I really a dick tease? I grabbed my jacket and walked across the quad, to his room and knocked on the door.

"WHAT?" He yelled when he opened it. I saw some chick sitting on his bed, fixing her clothes.

"Obviously, nothing." I went to walk away and he grabbed my arm.

"Get out, yo." He said to the chick and she looked at him weird.

"It's fine, we're done anyway." She grabbed her things.

"It's not even worth it." I had no clue what she spoke of, nor did I care at the moment. I was pissed. He's supposed to be my man and had another woman, in his room. I can't tell you if they had sex, because the covers were made and I didn't smell anything. People say, there's a sex smell but like I said, I didn't smell anything.

"Why you here Rak?" I hated when he called me that. It only sounded sexy coming out of Marco's mouth.

"I came to talk to you but it looks like you were busy."

"Man, we were doing work." He came closer to me.

"If we fucked, don't you think my bed would've been messed up or something?" I stared to see if he was lying. It didn't seem like he was, so I made myself comfortable.

"Is your roommate coming in tonight?" I asked because if we're about to do this, I don't need anyone, busting in or taping us.

"Nah, why?" I locked the door and stood in front of him. I removed my shirt, kicked off my Ugg slippers and slid my pants down. I stood there in my bra and panty set. The longer he stared, the more uncomfortable I got. I went to the bed and hurried to cover myself up.

"Damn, Rakia." He licked his lips and took the covers off.

"I thought you were bleeding."

"Ugh, I checked and it was over." I forgot, it's the reason he left in the first place.

"I'm not as experienced as other women, so please don't expect me to do too much."

"I can tell and I wouldn't do you like that." He took his clothes off and I closed my eyes. If I saw his penis, I'd probably stop.

He climbed on top of me and started kissing over my body. It felt more like he was slamming them on, instead of being gentle. He moved down to my private area, started to lick and I tried to get into it but couldn't. His tongue and mouth was all over the place. He continued until he thought I came and moved up to kiss me. I wasn't comfortable with this at first but Marco told me, never be ashamed of my body. They're my juices and if a man can taste them, I should too.

I felt him open my legs with his knee and tensed up a little. The only man to touch me was Marco and right now, I wanted to get up and run home to him. I wanted to let him make love to me but here I am, with Zaire. I heard him moan a little and then, he began moving in and outta me. I didn't feel a push or any pain. Did it mean, my vagina was very open? Oh my God, what if he thinks, I'm a hoe? I was so embarrassed, yet, he didn't say a word and continued grunting. I was about to ask to get on top, when he made a loud noise and fell on the side of me. *This can't be real.*

I may not be experienced but I do know, this sex session wasn't longer than three minutes because I looked at the alarm clock on his desk, right before he entered me. He laid his arm across my stomach and asked if I wanted some more. Of course, I did but the real questions is, do I want it from him? I shook my head yes and he asked me to use my mouth to get him hard again. Now he was bugging. I've never sucked a dick and he definitely won't be the first man, I try it on.

"I've never done that and I'm not ready anyway." He looked up at me and smiled.

"It's a first time for everything."

"Huh?" He stood up in front of me and used his hand to stoke his dick. Now, I'm thinking he didn't need help but that was far from the case.

"Just put your mouth around it and suck." Didn't I just tell him, I wasn't doing it? I sat up with the sheet wrapped around me and tried to move, to get my things. He yanked me by the hair.

"Suck it Rakia."

"No and get off my hair." I tried to move his hands off and he pushed me closer to his penis.

"Stop Zaire."

"I ate your pussy and you need to return the gesture."

"I didn't ask you too and no I'm not." I felt him move my head closer and I shut my mouth, tight.

"SUCK IT NOW!" He yelled and tears started coming down my eyes. I shook my head no and made an attempt to push him away. This time he grabbed my face with one hand, squeezed my cheeks so tight, my mouth opened and rammed his dick inside. He held his hand there and moved in and out my mouth. No matter, how hard I tried to escape his grasp, I couldn't.

"Shit, Rakia. I'm about to cum." He pumped faster. His hand let go of my face and outta nowhere, I felt something go in my mouth and his dick went soft. I instantly vomited and fell to the floor.

"Now, go. I need to sleep." I felt my clothes being tossed at me.

In this very moment, I felt violated, ashamed and most of all hurt. Hurt; that the man who claimed he was falling for me and had spent so much time with me, felt the need to force me to give him oral sex. How could he do that to me? I removed the sheet from my body and started to get dressed.

Right now, I didn't have the time or energy, to ask or figure it out on my own. He laid in the bed and shouted for me to hurry up. I stared at him in disbelief. This isn't the same man, who treated me like a queen, from the moment we met. He and I, were inseparable on campus at one point and now, he's showing a side, I didn't think, I'd ever see from any man.

I rushed to get dressed and he was on his phone, well I thought he was, until he turned it around and showed a video of him, making me suck his dick. When the hell did he record us and did he tape everything? I was so busy, locking the door and trying to give him what he wanted, I never took the time out to see exactly where his phone was. Why would he do this to me?

"Zaire, why would you tape us? Why would you force me to perform that on you?" I started crying harder.

"You wanted to be a woman, so I showed you what being one, is about."

"Zaire, you made me. That's not showing me."

"You have your way of looking at it and I have mine. Now go, so I can sleep. My class is early tomorrow."

"Are you going to walk me?"

"For what? You came over here on your own in the dark." I stared at him and opened the door. I guess, this is what I get for not speaking to Marco. Is this karma for me? And if it is, why do I have karma on me? I'm a good person but I guess, not everyone views me, as I view myself. I slammed his door and began walking down the hall. My body was pushed against the wall.

"Don't slam my fucking door." He had his hands on the top of my shirt.

"Yo, back the fuck up, off her."

"Mind yo business, bro. This between me and my girl." I don't even know who the guy was but he damn sure wasn't backing down from Zaire.

"Well, your girl looks petrified so I'd say, she isn't feeling the way you have her yoked up either."

"Tell him you're fine, Rakia." I saw the dude staring at me. Next thing I know, a few more guys came out their rooms and stood there.

"Do we have a problem?" Some other dude said and walked right up on him.

"Nah, we good." He let me go and pushed me down the hall but not without following me out. *Oh now, he wants to walk me across the quad.*

"We're watching you bro. If you lay one hand on her, that's your ass." I turned around and said thank you, to them.

"You think the shit is cute?"

"I didn't do anything Zaire. You're acting crazy over me slamming your door."

"We'll talk about this tomorrow. Go inside." He left me in the middle of the quad. I kept going, turned around at the door, only to catch him speaking to some chick and walking inside with her. I shook my head and went to my room. It's time for me to leave all men alone and I'm starting today.

Marco

It's been over a month since Rak, caught me in the truck with one of the other chicks, I fuck with. Hell yea, I was mad she told me to leave and that it's over. I brought my ass to the club, got drunk and once the chick said, she wanted some dick, she got it. In other people's eyes, it may not be right but there's no time limit when you break up with someone and sleep with the next. Am I in love with Rakia? Absolutely, but I'm not about to play any back and forth games with her either.

I wanted her to be my girl, which is why, after the block party, I had my computer guy find out her information and called her up at school. At first, she was standoffish but a few days of speaking to one another, she opened up a lot. The history on her family is a bit much and heartbreaking. You have her parents on drugs, her cousin despises her, her grandparents were mean and the only one in her corner when around, was her other cousin Rahmel; who I pulled a gun on. No wonder she picked a school far away.

When Cara's hateful ass blasted me about being out with Bobbi, it was for her own selfish intentions. The crazy part is, I didn't even take Bobbi shopping, nor did I kiss her. I was actually picking up some outfits for Rak to take back to school with her and Bobbi happened to catch me walking out. Even though, she told me on Thanksgiving she wasn't ready, I still found myself doing things for her. As far as, the kiss Cara spoke of; Bobbi, noticed her staring and planted one on my mouth. I almost cursed her the fuck out, until she pointed to her. I don't do that kissing in public shit unless you're my girl, and that she isn't. I guess being smart in front of Cara backfired because the bitch shouted it out.

I've been texting Rak, to check on her but she doesn't respond. After two weeks, I said fuck it and started doing me. She wants me to sit around waiting for her to make a decision and that ain't happening. I understand this is her first relationship and basically; her first at anything dealing with a man but damn. The minute we slept together and I made her my girl, nothing previously I did, should've even mattered because we weren't official.

"What you thinking about?" One of the strippers asked as she danced in front of me.

"Nothing. Keep dancing." I lifted my drink and continued watching her twerk. I never understood why men became infatuated with a woman doing it. Yea, it looks good but its overrated now.

"Can I go home with you daddy?" I smirked because I expected nothing else.

"HELL NO!" Bobbi stood in front of her. Moments like this, I should've taken her to VIP. Sometimes I wanted to mingle with the crowd but shit like this pissed me off.

"Bobbi, why you here?" I hadn't spoken to her, since the day at the mall. The chick, Rakia caught me with is someone else, I fucked with. Don't get it twisted now. My ass may be out here doing me but a nigga stayed strapped up.

"Marco, lets go."

"I'm not finished getting my dance. When I'm ready, I'll let you know." I pulled Bobbi down and made her wait. Yea, I'ma fuck her. It's what she wants and the reason she's blocking.

I allowed the chick to dance for a few more songs, then had her and a few others come over and put on a show, for some of the guys who work for me. Those niggas were losing their mind, watching all the tities and ass shake in front of them. Bobbi, looked aggravated but I didn't give a fuck. She's on my motherfucking time. I took a walk to the bathroom and ran straight into Tech.

"Yo, I've been calling you."

"What's up?" He said he'd wait for me to come out the bathroom. I tossed the paper towel in the trash and walked out, to see him standing there arguing with Shana.

"Why am I fired Tech?" I stood there listening.

"You tried to come for my wife and I told you before, she's off limits."

"Your wife? When the fuck did you get married?"

"None of your fucking business. Like I said, you should've never tried to come for her."

"Tech, she spit in my face." I busted out laughing. Ang, nasty as hell for doing some shit like that.

"Nobody told you to bring your ass to our table and you know damn well, you were there to start trouble. Fuck, out my face." He turned to walk away and this crazy bitch pushed him against the wall. *Wrong move!*

"I'm sorry Tech." She tried apologizing but it was too late. He had her against the wall, in the air barely breathing. His hands gripped her throat so bad, you could see her turning blue.

"Alright bro. Its too many people in here."

"Nah. Fuck this bitch. She thinks because we fucked, she could try me. Bitch, you're not my wife so don't ever put your hands on me." He dropped her and she hit the floor, hard as hell. He was about to kick her but I shoved him out the door. You could see people staring but no one said a word.

"You crazy as hell. Let me find out Ang, be whooping your ass." We both started laughing.

"I didn't mean it like that. I was saying she had no business touching me period."

"Whatever you say. I'm not judging."

"Fuck you. Ang, ain't crazy."

196

"She was crazy enough to leave your ass for three months though."

"I know. Yo, she was on some other shit but her ass locked down now. What's up with Rak? Have you spoken to her?"

"Nah. I reached out and she ignored me so I left her alone. I'm not sure us being together, is good anyway." He looked at me.

"It seems like she believes anything someone tells her and I can't deal with no insecure, chick."

"I feel ya."

"I'm not saying if she wanted to try again, I wouldn't. I'm saying she needs to seriously think about being with me. I'm a different type of nigga."

The two of us stood out there talking a little longer. He came to find me, to tell me they still don't know who the dude is, from the club. All we knew, was where he came from. Whoever he was, must not have known who we were because he pulled a suicide stunt in there. He screamed punk though. Who leaves right after they get knocked out? I expected him to come back, after he woke up and start some shit but nope; those niggas got the fuck outta dodge. Its all good though because he won't stay hidden forever and once his identity is confirmed, we'll be right at his doorstep.

"Marco, you ready?" Tech looked at me, when Bobbi walked out.

"Yea, get in your car." She did like I asked and Tech gave me a crazy look.

"What?" I shrugged my shoulders.

"Nothing man. Make sure you strap up. That bitch will try hard as hell for you to get her pregnant."

"I already know. Shit, I fuck her and everyone else with two condoms."

"What about Rak?"

"She'll never feel no condom on this dick. I'm always running up in her shit raw. And she was a virgin. You already know, I'm about to get her pregnant."

"You shot the fuck out."

"I'm serious. Whether we're together or not, I got that pussy on lock."

"So, you don't think she fucking at school?" He stood there with his arms folded.

"Why? What you heard?"

"Man, I ain't hear shit and you know Ang, won't tell. I'm just saying, since she's over you, and no longer a virgin, she may be dipping."

"If she is, I better not find out."

"Nigga, you said, she may not be the one for you."

"True but that pussy still mine." I chucked up the deuces and walked to the truck.

"Bye nigga. Text me when you get to the house so I know you made it. Crazy motherfucker." I heard him shout. I closed the door and had the driver take me to my condo.

I laid my head back and thought about what he said. What if Rak, is fucking someone else? I can't get mad but I will. She better not allow another nigga in between her legs. I know, its hypocritical of me but we all know, it's a double standard with women. Say what you want; and ready or not, Rak belongs to me. I may have to wait a few years for her to grow up but until then, I'm gonna knock her ass up.

Rakia

"Hi, can I get a plan B, please?" The woman behind the counter smiled and went to get it. After going in my room and thinking about everything that transpired with Zaire, it dawned on me, that we may not have used protection. I never heard a wrapper being opened and he came, when he got off me.

"Honey, before I give this to you, can I see some ID?" I handed it over.

"You let him cum in you?" I turned around and it was the same chick, I ran into at his dorm.

"Ummm."

"Can I help you ma'am?"

"No. Don't you see me speaking to her?" She was an older black woman and not beat for this girl's shit.

"I see you being fucking nosy, is what I see. Whatever man, this woman slept with is none of your business. Now, if you don't want anything in this store, I suggest you take your tacky ass, the fuck up outta here."

"How you cussing at customers?"

"The same way, you're in this woman's business."

"I should tell the manager on you."

"Go ahead."

"Where is he?"

"I'm standing right here, boo." The woman pointed to her shirt and it clearly read, store manager on it. I didn't pay attention to it, which means she didn't either. The girl stood there looking stupid as hell.

"You're a dumb bitch, anyway. I told you he wasn't worth fucking before I left the room, last night. I bet he came in less than five minutes. He's a minute man love and the only reason, I sleep with him, is for the money."

"Excuse me! Sleep with him. How are you sleeping with him, when he's my man?" She laughed harder and I could see the woman coming from behind the counter.

"Honey, I've been sleeping with him for two years."

"Two years? How, when we're always together? I've never seen you before and.-" I felt myself rambling and then a hand on my shoulder.

"This is the problem with women now." She told me to relax and never let a woman see you sweat.

"If you knew he had a woman, why continue to sleep with him? And if you've been with him for two years and he's only giving you money and still hasn't made you his woman, I'd look into that. It's obvious, you're not good enough to be seen on his arm, which is why he keeps you on call for pussy. Honey, you are way too pretty to be a ho." The woman said and the chick was fuming.

"I ain't no ho."

"I'm trying to be nice and not call you a prostitute but the fact is, a woman who gets paid to have sex, is exactly that. Now again, if you're not getting anything, I suggest you leave." The manager stood in front of the chick and she stormed out.

"Thank you miss. I'm not confrontational and.-"

"You don't have to explain yourself, love. I can't stand for women to try and belittle another; especially over a man, who's obviously is using them."

"Do you think she's lying about them sleeping together?"

"Honey, the question is; do you think she's lying? You're the one who's been with this man."

"I know but how could I tell? He's always with me, unless its time to go to bed. I don't allow him to stay the night with me."

"Then, believe what she said. If he isn't sleeping with you, then he's been with others. Now, I'm not saying all men cheat and some of her story could be false but I've learned that, no woman will approach you with all lies. Some of what they say, will be true but its up to you, to decipher which part is." We heard some people come in and she hurried to place the item in my bag. She grabbed my hand after handing me the change.

"I can tell you're not from around here so if you ever need someone to talk to, give me a call." She handed me a card and walked away. I'm going to call her too. I hope she can answer my questions.

****

Three days went by and I hadn't heard from Zaire, which is a good thing; however, something is wrong down in my private area. I've been having a really bad itch and it's been uncomfortable, using the bathroom. I went to the medical office they have here and the nurse refused to check me because she said, it may be something, she couldn't expose the office to and sent me down to an Urgent care clinic. I had no money left, to do so and called my aunt to ask if she could Western Union me some money. She told me no, and hung up the phone. I was shocked because she's always given me what I asked for; maybe she was over it. I ended up contacting my grandmother and she told me to, use the check she gave me. I was scared to tell her, I lost it but I had no choice,

"RAKIA, HOW DID YOU LOSE THE CHECK?"

"Grandma, I left it at the house the day you gave it to me. It was hidden under my bed, but when I checked, it was gone. I'm sorry, I didn't tell you. Please don't be mad."

"What have you been doing for money?"

"Nothing. I grab extra food during the week, for the weekend so I don't starve. I had some money from Rahmel but

204

it ran out, a few days ago. I really don't need anything else." I used my last $50 on the Plan B but I'd never tell her that.

"Rakia, you're in college now. You will always need items. What about personal stuff?"

"I have all that and if I run out, the medical office will give me some." She blew her breath out.

"Rakia, I'm gonna send you $300, to Western Union. Then, I'm gonna go to the bank and have them issue me another check. If you lost the other one, they'll see it wasn't cashed and give me a new one."

"Thank you, grandma."

"Before I go, what's this money for?" I was so embarrassed. I told her and she cursed me out so bad, I started crying. She asked, how could I be stupid and the guy most likely, gave me something.

"Please don't tell anyone."

"I'm not and I'm gonna ask Shanta, why she couldn't send you something? She used to give you money all the time."

"Its ok grandma. I don't want any issues. I'm going to wait at Western Union and thanks again." We said our goodbyes and hung up.

I grabbed my purse and walked the two miles, to get to the place and wait for her to send it. It was nippy out but I had to do, what I had to. My grandma sent me a text and said it was sent. I received the money and took an Uber to the clinic. It wasn't too crowded for a Saturday. I gave my information and reason for being there and took a seat.

I couldn't stop the itch in my private area and caught myself scratching harder than normal. Some woman looked at me, shaking her head. Someone called my name and I damn near ran to the back. A nurse took my vitals and told me not to get undressed. The doctor came in and closed the door. She introduced herself and grabbed a pair of gloves.

"Unfortunately; Ms. Winters, due to your description of why you came here, I won't be able to perform and exam on you. However, I am going to take a look." I went to undo my jeans and she stopped me.

"Ms. Winters, please don't."

"But how can you look?"

"I'm going to lower the top of your jeans, just above the panty line. If you have what I think you do, I can't expose this room." I nodded and waited for her to do it. She lifted my jeans and told me to stand up.

"Ok, Ms. Winters, it's as I expected."

"What do you mean?" She sat at the desk and started writing on a blue pad.

"Honey, you have contracted pubic lice, which others may call, crabs. The other symptoms you informed me of, could be a case of gonorrhea, chlamydia or syphilis." I had to grab onto the bed, to hold myself up. There's no way, I could have an STD! Yes, I was careless, but Zaire wouldn't give me anything, would he?

"Here is a prescription for RID. Its and over the counter medication. Once, you get it, make sure it says for pubic lice and read the directions carefully. Also, because I can't do an exam, I'm going to prescribe you Azithromycin, in case you do have one of the STD's, I mentioned. I am giving you a penicillin shot as well."

"How could I let this happen?"

"Sweetie, this happens to a lot of women. I will say for future reference, make sure the man uses a condom." She left out and returned with a kit, containing a needle and medication. She had me lower the back of my jeans a little and jammed it, in the side of my ass. I almost cried from the pain.

"The blood work my nurse took, should be back in a few days. I'll contact you with the results and Ms. Winters." I looked at her.

"Refrain from sex for two weeks so the medicine can work properly and whoever the man is, who gave you this, needs to be notified as well so he can be treated."

"I can't tell him. He'll think I gave it to him."

"Did you?"

"No. He's only the second person, I've slept with. I had an abortion not too long ago, and my health was fine."

"Well, if you don't want to tell him. Send him a letter or something. Keep it anonymous but its only right to make sure he knows."

"But.-"

"I know, he should've told you but he may not have known." I nodded my head and grabbed everything she gave me. I felt like an idiot and most of all, I was disgusted with myself for allowing him to give me a disease. Shit, Marco didn't even give me one and I know he had hoes.

I went straight to the pharmacy, picked up the items and left. I was happy the store manager wasn't there because she'd probably rip into me about it. I sat at my desk, typed up a letter to Zaire, placed it in an envelope and walked across the quad, to his dorm. I knew he wasn't there because he always went home every other weekend. I slid it under his door and ran back to my room.

I grabbed the RID stuff and went to shower. Since it was late, no one was in the bathroom. I opened the box and followed the directions. Standing there waiting for these things to fall off, was driving me crazy. I didn't have a lot of hair down there but enough to slide the comb through. I almost threw up, seeing these things on the comb and cried the entire time.

After I finished, I opened the small container of bleach, poured it on the floor and wiped down the walls and floor of the shower. I tried not to infect anyone and the only things, I know that got rid of everything, is bleach or ammonia. I couldn't use ammonia due to the strong smell, so this would have to do. Someone came in when I finished and said she was happy the people came to clean the bathroom because it was disgusting. If she only knew, the shower is the only thing I did. But she was right, women were nasty.

I left out, went to my room and gathered all my clothes, towels, bedding and even the set of curtains I had and went down to the laundry room. I placed them in the washer, in hot water and stayed down there until the cycle was over; only to re wash the stuff two more times. The dryer was placed on extra hot to make sure they were gone. I didn't go to bed until after four in the morning and I only used a sheet to sleep in. The directions told me to repeat the process the next day, and I didn't want to wash everything again.

I got outta bed the next day, at six to get in the shower before everyone else. It was Sunday, so I knew there wouldn't be anyone awake. I looked at myself, when I did the RID again and nothing came off, this time. I guess, I did a good job scrubbing them off and then shaving, last night. Once I finished, I repeated the process with the bleach and went to my room. I made my bed and started to feel a little better about being clean. I prayed, this never happened to me again.

Cara

When my mom told Rakia no, about sending money, two weeks ago, I was shocked. She usually gave her whatever she wanted. I'm sure she had no idea, I was listening but the curiosity in me, made me go ask her why. At first, she refused to answer but after asking again, she broke down and told me why.

"How could your cousin, choose him over you?" I smiled because, I was finally getting my mother back.

"I don't know mommy. I tried to tell her we slept together, about the loss of my child and you see how that went. She didn't even care, when I told her he put a knife to my throat. It's like she'll only believe whatever he tells her."

"Cara, you should've told her sooner."

"I did ma. I talked to her a lot, when she first left but she still slept with him. I didn't wanna tell you this but she's been after him, ever since I staked claim on him."

"What you mean?" My mom sat up on the bed.

"A little over a year ago, we saw him at the bodega. He was hitting on me and afterwards she told me, he was cute. Now, you've always told us, whoever saw the guy first, gets first dibs and we have to back off."

"Right."

"Well, I saw him at the bodega and remember those two nights, I told you about in New York?" she nodded her head.

"I was with him."

"WHAT?" She stood up and began pacing back and forth. I was truly getting a kick outta lying. FUCK THAT! If I can't have him and live my dream, of being with a baller, then she damn sure won't either. I promise to fuck up anything she thinks, she may have with him. I'm not about to be outdone by my retarded ass cousin.

"Yup, we had sex and have been since then."

"Well, you need to stay away from him and as far as Rakia; I'll deal with her. She was raised better than that." She left the house and walked down to my grandmothers. I'm sure, she's going to discuss perfect Rakia, with her. If I wasn't already going to the mall, I'd go with her.

Tonight, there was a big party at Tech's club, for Marco's birthday. I mean, any and everyone was supposed to be in attendance. I also heard, a few rappers are supposed to be there but I couldn't tell you which ones. There were so many out these days, it was hard to keep up. All I know is, a bitch would be there, dressed to impress and if anyone thought about trying to ruin my shine, I'd make sure they'd regret it.

****

I was in the mall minding my own business, when I overheard some chick saying, she couldn't wait to get Marco home tonight. She had so many surprises for him; including a threesome. Now a bitch like me, wanted to be down so I made my way over to where she was and continued listening. She wanted to find someone who would be able to move on after the sex and not try and stick around. Of course, I threw on my famous smile and offered my services.

"Have you ever been in a threesome?" I was shocked, she didn't ask why I listened to her phone call.

"No, but how hard could it be?" She hung the phone up and pulled me outside.

"A threesome, requires two women to perform on one another, as well as with the guy. Have you ever ate a woman's pussy, or had yours eaten by one?"

"Again, it can't be that hard." She smirked.

"You're right. It's not and I'm sure you taste good." She licked her lips and as awkward as it was, I was slightly turned on. Little did she know, I ain't putting my mouth on her. I planned on slipping her something and having Marco, to myself.

"Gimmie your number and I'll call your after we leave so you can meet us." I gave it to her and went on about my way. A bitch was in her glory, until I ran into these ho's.

"Hey Cara?" Rakia spoke and hugged me. I stared at her and caught an attitude. She had her hair done really nice and I could see her feet and nails were freshly done.

"Hey! What are you doing in town?"

"Oh. I'm off for summer break. I came this morning on the train." I forgot, she totaled her truck and had no transportation.

"Umm hmm. Damn Angela, it looks like you're still pregnant."

"CARA!" Rakia shouted.

"What? She does? How many months are you?"

"You know, I had my son." She gave me a fake smile. I did know because I ran into her at the grocery store, with her mother. Her mom was talking to me about some nonsense. I asked her then, the same question. I also, noticed the big ass rock on her finger, that I didn't see the other day. I lifted her hand and admired the hell outta it. The shit had to be expensive as hell.

"Its huge, right?" Rakia asked.

"I guess, if you like small diamonds." I was hating and she knew it. The diamond was nowhere near small.

"Cara, that diamond is huge."

"If you say so. Who did you get married to?" Both of them looked at me crazy.

"What? I heard Tech, let some stripper suck his dick, so I know it ain't him." I shrugged my shoulders. The stripper Shana, told everyone she stole Tech from her. At first, I didn't believe her but then, I would see him around and she was nowhere in sight; not even for the holidays. I figured it was true.

"Cara, why are you being mean to Angela?"

"Its ok Rakia." Ang smiled.

"See, Cara wants everyone around, to be as miserable as, she is. I'm gonna let you in on a secret Cara." She stepped in my face.

"Tech, has and will never be any of your concern but if you must know, he is my husband." I rolled my eyes.

"I see you in your feelings but I'm not pregnant now and will fuck you up, if you even think about coming out your face with something else, disrespectful."

"Ang, I don't want you two fighting. Come on, ladies. I've been away for almost a year and we should go party, or have lunch."

"I'm busy." I pushed past them.

If the bitch shows up at the party, I'm gonna make sure she regrets it. I'm sure Ang, told her about it. Tonight, is my night with Marco and no one is standing in my way and I mean it.

****

"We'll be leaving the club after two, so stay around." The girl said on the phone.

I acknowledged her statement and went to my car, to hit the club. It was a hoopty, but it got me where I needed to. Shit, since my cousin didn't have a ride, it was no need to ask her to bring me.

I parked around the corner from the club and walked. The line was ridiculous and security was everywhere. People were being checked and I didn't see Trey anywhere. I called and as usual, he let me go straight in. If Tech or Marco, knew he did this favor for me, they'd probably fire him.

The club was already full and I could see people starting to go upstairs to the other bar area. Tech had an extra area for huge events like this because he knew, the crowd would be overwhelming. I only know because the chick, who

I'm supposed to do the threesome with told me. She said, they'll be in VIP and that the other portion of the club would be open and told me to stay close. When Marco leaves, they usually make everyone stay inside, until he's in his ride and pulling off. I swear, they treated him like a damn celebrity and I loved it. I planned on fucking him real good tonight, so he'll have me next to him at the next party.

The night was going well and I received a few phone numbers. Around midnight, the DJ had everyone sing happy birthday to him and he thanked them all. Shortly after, some guy named Travis Scott came out, then another guy named 21 Savage and a few others. The crowd was going wild.

It wasn't until after one, when I noticed them walking in. Rakia had on a skin tight, cream colored dress with some red bottoms, Ang probably let her borrow. And Ang, wore a skin tight red dress and some red bottoms too. I thought she was bigger in the mall but I guess the baggy clothes disguised a lot. Ang, had a snap back body and I was hating for sure.

Some niggas tried to talk to her but she waved them off. Rakia, on the other hand went on the dance floor and I knew then, my night would be ruined, if he saw her. I sent a text message to the chick and told her we should leave now. I looked up and she had a scowl on her face looking down on the dance floor. Her glare met mine and she gestured for me, to meet her in the bathroom.

"If he's sees her, we can forget about tonight." The girl was nervous as hell.

"Who?" I played dumb to make sure we were both talking about my cousin.

"The bitch, he thought he loved. Rakia, or some shit." She had anger in her voice.

"Look, I'm gonna tell him it's time to get his surprise. Be ready." She stepped out and left me in there. The stall opened and out walked Angela, laughing.

"What?"

"You two are so threatened by Rakia, that you're willing to make this man, leave his own party, just so he won't see her. Let me fill you in on something though."

"What?" I had my hands on my hips.

"She doesn't want him."

"Then why is she here?" She tossed the paper towel and started applying lipstick.

"Because I invited her. My husband is working and I didn't want to sit alone."

"Whatever."

"Honey, you need to stop stressing over Rakia and get a life. She's moved on from Marco and you should too." She put her lipstick on and went to the door.

"Have a good night." She left and I was right behind her. Tonight, better go my way, or someone is going to pay, dearly.

Marco

"Happy Birthday, bro." Tech handed me a bottle of Ace of Spades, a big gift bag and an envelope. Ang, made him buy me a gift; even though, I told her we don't do that shit.

"Make sure, I thank Ang, later."

"Yo, how you know I didn't get it."

"Because we don't do gifts, bro. I know, she made you do it." We both laughed. I opened the Rolex, the Louis Vuitton slippers, belt, glasses and the envelope with a 100k in it."

"I told her no."

"Nah man. I appreciate it. If anything, I know the cash is from you." We gave each other a hug and took a few shots together.

"Oh, your other surprise is here." He had a smirk on his face.

"Man, you didn't have to do that."

"I think, this is a surprise you'll wanna take home right away." He left me standing there and Bobbi walked back over.

A few minutes ago, she had an attitude about something and all of a sudden, she's happy.

"I'm ready for our threesome baby. And I have to tell you, she's gorgeous."

"Word!" I licked my lips. She knew, I loved having sex with multiple women at once. The way, they devoured one another and then me, always had me down for whatever.

"Alright. Let me tell Tech, I'm out."

"NO!" She shouted, when I went to leave the area.

"What the fuck is wrong with you? You know, we don't leave without letting the other one know."

"Can't you send him a text? I mean, you do wanna see me in action." I had a grin on my face and walked over to her.

"Damn, you want me real bad."

"Always." I picked up my bag and started walking out the private door with her but stopped when security pointed behind me. I heard Bobbi suck her teeth and I couldn't blame her. She knew, how I felt about Rakia, who stood there nervous as hell, next to Tech and Ang. Those two, were feeling each other up, like the perverts they are. Ever since they've been married, he hasn't thought about another woman. I was honestly happy for him.

"Rak?" She smiled and came towards me. I saw her stop, when Bobbi swooped her arms in mine.

"I'm sorry. I didn't know you were with someone." I moved Bobbi's arm and grabbed her, before she could leave.

"Damn, I really missed you." I pulled her close and hugged her tight. I didn't wanna let go and she didn't make me.

"I'm ready Marco." I heard Bobbi yelling.

"I came to say Happy Birthday. I don't want to interrupt so I'll see you around."

"Fuck her. How long are you home for?"

"Summer break. But I'm going back in August, to get a head start."

"Look at my scholar student. Always being two steps ahead of everyone." She blushed and put her head down. I lifted it back up with my index finger, under her chin.

"Stay with me tonight."

"Marco." I could see her fighting it.

"Please." I never beg but I'd do it for her.

"Marco, why are you tryna get her to stay with you? She already aborted the baby you put in her. It's obvious she doesn't wanna have anything to do with you." I moved her away from me. Ang and Tech, both looked at her, which told me, they didn't know either.

"What is she talking about Rakia?" I had no idea, she was pregnant by me. It was definitely possible because I never wore a condom with her.

"Marco, can we discuss this somewhere else?" I could see her eyes getting watery.

"Tell me right fucking now. Did you abort my kid?"

"Marco, please."

"Yo, get her the fuck outta here right now, before I do something, I won't regret."

"Marco."

"BITCH, DON'T SAY MY NAME."

"Hold up Marco. I know, you're upset but don't talk to her like that." Ang said and all I could do was turn to leave. I loved Ang like my sister and I know Rakia, is like hers. I also, know my temper and if I didn't bounce, I'd probably disrespect her too. I respected Tech too much, for us to be beefing."

"You were just asking me to leave with you and the minute she said something to you, I'm a bitch. Marco, I would and have never, called you out your name, regardless of how bad you hurt me. You won't even let me explain and automatically say, fuck me." Rakia yelled. She followed me through the private door, I took her in, when we first met. The next thing she said, pissed me the fuck off.

"I'm glad, I got rid of it because I could never have a baby with a man, who's a baby himself." I ran up on her and Tech blocked me.

"Was I a baby, when I fucked the shit outta you? Huh? Was I a baby, when I taught.-"

"That's enough Marco." Ang said and grabbed a distraught Rakia away from me. At that moment, I knew, I fucked up. Not only did I disrespect the shit outta her, I was about to tell everyone she was a virgin. How could I get this angry over a chick? I knew, I was in love with her back then but was I still in love?

"Bro, that was fucked up."

"I don't wanna talk about it. I'll see you tomorrow." I got in the truck and had the driver take me to the house Bobbi, assumed, I lived at. Yea, I'm always here but my residence is where, Rakia and I, were at.

"Who told you she had an abortion?" I stared out the window.

"Huh?"

"Don't huh me. Who told you she had an abortion?" She swallowed hard before speaking.

"She posted something on Instagram about going to a clinic and making a hard decision, but it was best for her. I put two and two together." Nothing she said made sense, so I left it alone for now.

When we pulled up, there was a hoopty down the street. I didn't say anything and had my guards go check it out. I slammed my keys on the counter and went upstairs to get in the shower. A few minutes later, I could hear two chicks in the room talking and called Bobbi in the bathroom. I told her, I wasn't feeling this but she promised it would be worth it.

227

I finished washing up, stepped out the shower and heard moaning. The room was dim and I couldn't really see, who the other chick was but it didn't matter. My dick was hard looking at Bobbi devour the shit outta her. I picked up a condom and plunged right inside Bobbi.

"Shit, I'm cumming." I thought, I knew the voice of the chick and was about to go off, until Bobbi turned around and caught my nut. I fell on the bed and the chick moved down, to where my dick was and began sucking it. Right then, I knew exactly who it was because she still had no clue what to do. I pushed her off and grabbed another condom. Since, this is what she's been dying to get, a nigga is about to bless her.

I turned her over and rammed myself inside. She almost jumped off the bed. I pulled out to make sure, the condom wasn't ripped and continued fucking the hell outta her. I started to get aggravated, from all the yelling she was doing and Bobbi knew. She handed me a new condom and took her place. Bobbi had her sit cowgirl style on her face. Shorty, had a nice ass but she couldn't handle dick, well; not mine, anyway. I fucked Bobbi until she came. Shorty, tried to get me to fuck her again but it wasn't happening. I already fucked up, doing it in the first place.

"Get the fuck out, yo." I threw the clothes at her, snatched her up by the arm and dragged her down the steps. I stood there while she put them on.

"Why wouldn't you fuck me again?"

"I should've never fucked you in the first place and trust, it won't happen again."

"Marco, can't you see, I'm the woman for you?" I busted out laughing.

"There's only one woman for me and she ain't here. Get the fuck on." I opened the door.

"Oh, your precious Rakia. The chick, who's killing babies and shit." I figured she would know and probably the one, who told Bobbi.

"A baby, you tried to get from me too, huh? Bitch, I saw you try and pop the rubber, which is why, I made her give me the other one."

"What?" When Bobbi was eating her pussy, she must didn't know, I was out the shower yet. I saw her reach over, on the nightstand where the condoms were and hold it in her hand.

I can't tell you what she was doing because like I said, it was

dark. Anyway, when Bobbi handed me the condom to fuck her,

I threw it on the ground and made her give me another one.

One thing, I do, is always pay attention to my surroundings.

"The only person who has ever felt this dick raw, is

Rakia and it'll stay that way. Now, go."

"You may be right but the fact, I can brag about

fucking you for real this time, is enough to crush her soul." I

don't know why I let her get to me but I punched her in the

face and kept hitting her, until my guards pulled me off. That's

what I get for trying to hurt Rakia, for aborting my baby. I may

really have to pay this bitch to keep quiet now. *What the fuck?*

****

"Where's my godson?" I asked Tech, when he opened

the door.

"Right here, you nasty ass, nigga." Ang said and

handed him to me. I sucked my teeth and went in the living

room. I sat on the couch and laid him on my shoulder. I loved this little nigga as if he were mine. I think it's why I got angry hearing Rakia, got rid of my kid.

"Hey, lil man. We gonna have to teach you how to get all the ho's." Ang mushed me in the head and sat next to me. I swear, she be testing me but I won't ever hit her.

"You lucky, I love my brother and godson or I promise, I'd smack the hell outta you right now." She stuck her finger up.

"Why you play my girl out like that?"

"She should've told me."

"I can't argue with that. To be honest, I didn't even know. But what I do know, is something happened up at her school, and even though she's going back, she doesn't want to." I sat up.

"What you mean?"

"She came home yesterday and I could tell something was bothering her but each time I asked, she would say nothing. Then last night, on our way to drop her off, she kept rambling on."

"About what?"

"I couldn't make everything out. Marco, you know if you don't pay close attention, you'll miss what she's saying." I nodded. She was right. Rakia would ramble on so fast, you'd have to hang on every word to make sure, you caught it all.

"She mentioned some guy, who did bad things to her and wondered if it was her karma for not telling you something. I asked over and over, to repeat herself but she wouldn't. Rak, can be as smart as she wanna be, however; she can be very gullible and ditzy about other things. I'm telling you, shit ain't right up there at school." I was becoming upset, listening to her tell me, someone may have hurt her.

"Where is she now"

"Let her be."

"Nah, she needs to tell me what's going on." I handed her the baby and told Tech, I'd be back.

Ang, still refused to tell me where she was, so stopped at her grandmothers. I couldn't tell if she were here because she had no car. I made a call before getting out and told them, they better have one here in an hour, or else. The door opened, before I could knock and Shanta stood there with her arms folded. She had the nerve to look pissed, as if I gave a fuck.

"Where's Rak?" She closed the door and came on the porch.

"You got some nerve coming here."

"And why is that?" I pulled the mild off the side of my ear, lit it up and blew smoke in her face. I used to like her but she was telling my pops some bullshit and I wanted to see if she'd say it now. Yea, they started fucking around again, not too long ago.

"How dare you play these cousins against one another?"

"Say what now?"

"I've always taught them to have each other's back and if one of them, liked a guy, the other one, is supposed to back up. Then here you come along and Cara see's you first, stakes her claim on you and even spent two days in New York with you. Then, you flock to Rakia, sleep with her and leave Cara in the cold. And let's not discuss what went down with you and her, last night." I shook my head laughing.

"Let's get one thing straight Shanta. Cara, is a hateful, jealous and envious bitch and whether you admit it or not, you know it too. If you wanna know the truth, your ho ass daughter was in another nigga's face, the day at the bodega and Rakia, stood there staring at me, as I got out the truck. When I came out the store, that slut daughter of yours, tried to pop her pussy for me, even though she noticed Rakia, saw me first. So, you see, Cara has been filling your head up with these lies because she wants me and the feelings are not reciprocated. She can't handle me wanting Rakia and has told me on plenty of occasions, she's the better woman, oh and that she wants my kids." Shanta stood there with her mouth hanging open.

"As far as last night, the thot bitch, crept in my spot, with the other ho, I'm fucking and offered a threesome. She couldn't take the dick, I kicked her out, she said some shit to piss me off and I beat her ass." I blew more smoke in her face.

"Is there anything else you wanna know before, I go inside and speak to Rakia?"

"Does your father know, you speak about women this way?"

"Bitch, I'm a grown ass man."

"BITCH!"

"That's what I said, ain't it? Get the fuck out my face."
I pushed her to the side and opened the door. Her grandmother
was in the kitchen with a smirk on her face.

"I'll be back ma." Shanta yelled from the porch.

"I'm so glad you went off on her. She used to be down
for Rakia but now that her demon ass daughter spit all those
lies, she believes anything that leaves her mouth. Do you know
the little bitch, stole Rakia's money and tried to cash the
check?"

"What?" I was pissed, She started telling me about the
money, she saved up for her, from the time they took her from
the hospital, as a baby.

The reason she wasn't with Cara at the bank, when she
attempted to cash it, was because she claimed, Rakia was in the
car and would be right in. She walked out and never went back
in. She went on to say, the cops asked if she wanted to press
charges and Rakia asked her not to. I couldn't believe the
lengths this bitch was going through to hurt her. I knew about

the money because she had the check put in Rakia's name and when I had my boy do a background check on her, it popped up.

I asked if she knew what Rakia was going through at school and she told me to sit. She sat across from me and said, she wasn't sure but she did get into some trouble and she had to send her $300. I thought she'd tell me what but she didn't. She doesn't want Rak, to go back but she's hella bent on getting her engineering degree and wasn't letting anything stop her.

After sitting here for a while, I realized Rak, couldn't have been home. She would've come down the stairs by now because we were loud talking and joking about other things. My phone rang and the guy told me he was outside. I told her grandmother, I'd be right back, watched him take the truck off the flatbed and hand me the keys.

"Tell Rakia, I'll be back." I put the keys to a brand new 2018, Lexus truck in her hand. I had to get it in black and I hoped she liked it. It was the only one they had available, fully loaded.

"Marco, she needs help."

"Where is she?"

"Unfortunately, at the hospital with Cara."

"Bet."

"She told Rakia, you did it."

"It won't be the first time, she knew I laid hands on her. I'm sorry but Cara deserves every ass whooping I give her. I know she's a woman and I'd rather hit a man but she fucking with the right one. She's lucky, I didn't kill her in the hospital, when she lied to Rak." She nodded and went in the house. I hated cursing in front of her but she knew, I didn't give a fuck. Now, I had to find a way to speak to her, without seeing Cara. I hope she didn't mention, she was at my house.

Rakia

I was so hurt by the way Marco spoke to me, I tossed and turned half the night. Who did he think he was and who disclosed, my personal information to him? I told no one about the abortion, nor did I want him to find out the way he did. I had plans on telling him the next day because I refused to ruin his birthday. I knew he'd be upset but the way he behaved, is not at all, what I expected.

When my aunt Shanta came banging on the door, around three this morning, I had finally drifted off to sleep. Shanta said, Marco beat Cara up really bad and she was in the hospital. Why Cara pushed his buttons, is beyond me. Its' like she was doing it on purpose but why? Who wants to be laid up with black eyes, concussions and bruised ribs? Maybe, it's better for me to stay away from him. If he's doing this to her, I damn sure, don't ever wanna feel the pain she claims to be in. She could barely move and one of her eyes, was shut and swollen, like a baseball was in it.

****

I was dosing off in the chair at the hospital, when her mom came in screaming and asking why am I here. Now, I had no idea why she's upset or questioning anything. She left me here, to go by the house and get clothes for Cara, which took a lot longer than expected but she was aware, I was here. I stared at her and so did my cousin. I mean she was in here cursing and threatening me, as if I'm the one, who put Cara here. Instead of engaging her with questions, I quickly put my sneakers on and picked my purse and phone up to leave.

SMACK! SMACK! Is all you could hear as my aunt slapped the hell outta me. I've never been hit in my life. My grandparents were mean but never once, laid a hand on me.

"Ma, what are you doing?" I heard Cara ask, which shocked me.

"Fuck this bitch."

"AUNT SHANTA, STOP." I shouted, when she grabbed me by the hair and started punching me in the face. I felt her bang my head into the wall and I swore, it was over. It hurt really bad and yet, she was still hitting me.

"This will teach you not to sleep with a man, your cousin had eyes for, first. I taught you better than that. Now take this ass whooping." She continued raining blows on me. If I wanted to respond to what she was saying, I couldn't because I started going in and out of consciousness. I screamed for help, as much as, I could.

"HELP ME! SOMEONE PLEASE HELP ME!" I shouted and people came running in the room. My aunt had a death grip on my hair.

"Call security."

"Please stop aunt Shanta. Why are you hitting me?" I kept yelling out but she wouldn't let my hair go. Each time, I thought she stopped hitting me, I felt another one, on the opposite side.

"WHAT THE FUCK?" I heard and all of a sudden, my hair was released and she stopped. I laid on the ground, crying hysterical.

"Why the fuck you standing there? GET A FUCKING DOCTOR IN HERE, TO CHECK HER OUT!" He lifted me off the floor.

"Bitch, you fucked up, coming for my girl." I wrapped my arms around him. I couldn't believe he still considered me to be his girl. Especially after, the way he spoke to me, last night.

"Fuck her." Marco, stopped at the door and handed me, to one of his guards.

"Oh, you tough because we're in this hospital? Bitch, I will slice your fucking throat and watch your body drop, right here." He pulled the hunters knife, out his sock and put it to her throat. You could see the indent, as he pressed it hard, against her throat.

He told me before, the reason he kept it there, is in case his gun ever ran outta bullets and he needed something else. Tech once told me, Marco's knife skills are nothing to fuck with. He can toss it from across a parking lot and still, hit his target.

"Marco, please don't." Shanta backed up to the wall. I could tell he wanted to take her life, more than Cara's at the moment and here I was, begging him not to.

"That's your fucking niece, you stupid bitch. You get in your feeling because I told you how much of a ho, your daughter was and attack her. Everyone knows, she isn't a fighter and the sad part is, she's probably gonna forgive you after this but I won't. I'm coming for you bitch and there won't be a motherfucker who can hide you from me; not even my pops." He came back to me and kissed my lips.

"Where the fuck is the doctor?" One of the nurses pointed to a room, where the guy stood there; looking scared as hell. They went in with me and Marco, had the guard stand outside while the doctor examined me.

"She's gonna need an x-ray, of her ribs and a cat scan, of the head."

"That bitch kicked you?" He asked and I told him, I didn't know. Once she banged my head against the wall, everything else was blurry.

"There's a huge knot on the back of her head and one on the side, over here." He pointed and Marco looked. He picked his phone up and made a call.

"Is the nanny there?" Tech, must've said yes. I knew it was him, by their conversation.

"Do me a favor. Take Ang, over to Rak's grandmother's house and pick the truck up. I'll call and tell you, when I'm on my way home. I need you to meet me there with Ang. After this shit, she's gonna need her friend. I'll hit you, when we're done." He said and put the phone in his pocket.

"Marco, please don't leave me here. What if she comes back?" He grabbed my hand.

"I'm not going anywhere and I doubt you'll see her for a while and when you do, it'll be in a fucking coffin."

"Marco, please don't.-" I said and everything was black.

****

"Thank goodness, you're awake." My grandmother said and started rubbing my head.

"Grandma, I don't know why she attacked me." I started crying and heard beeping noises.

"Shhh. You can't worry about it. How are you feeling?" My grandmother, looked tired and I didn't like that.

243

"I'm fine. Are you ok?"

"Yea. I'm just worried about you." She gave me a hug and told me she was stepping outside because someone wanted to see me. I smiled as he stepped in, looking fresh to death.

"You scared me ma. Don't ever do that shit again." He pecked my lips.

"I'm sorry. What happened?"

"The knot on your head, had a clot in it and caused you to pass out. They had to do a small operation, to drain it. Your ribs were bruised and you have a black eye. Otherwise; you good, baby girl."

"Marco, let me explain, why I didn't tell you about the abortion."

"Not right now." I squeezed his hand.

"Please." He stood there and waited.

"Marco, I didn't know about the pregnancy, at first. When I did, I called your phone. Some chick answered and told me, never to contact you again. Of course, I did anyway and my calls continuously went to voicemail. I sent you a text message about it but you never responded. I called you, a day or two later and again, it was the same thing. I figured you moved on and should've been more careful about who you left your phone around. Marco, I tried to tell you so we could make the decision together. I didn't have a lot of time and I did, what I thought was best for both of us. I'm sorry."

"Nah, ma. I'm sorry, for snapping and not hearing you out. You're right about me being careful about who I leave my phone around. I didn't even know you were blocked. To know, you had to make a decision like that on your own, makes me feel like shit, for not checking on you. I understand, if you don't wanna talk to me for the way I behaved."

"I forgave you already, Marco."

"Word!"

"You know, I forgive easily and besides, I'm still in love with you."

"I'm still in love with you too." He leaned down and we engaged in a deep, erotic kiss."

"She's been sleep for two days nigga, let her breathe." Ang said, walking in. I had no idea, I was asleep that long.

245

"Tech, she got one more time." Marco said and we all started laughing.

"How are you sis?" She had tears coming down her eyes.

"Don't cry Ang. I'm ok."

"I'm gonna whoop her ass, when I find her."

"Please don't. I want all of you, to just forget it, please." Marco came over to where I was. He had walked out to use the phone.

"Ma, why do you keep forgiving the shit they do to you? I know, I fucked up but they've been doing this all your life, well; Cara has anyway. I'm not sure, what the hell is up with your aunt but she has it coming too. Baby, you have a big and forgiven heart but some people don't deserve to have you in their life and that's some real shit."

"Honestly, I don't know why? It's like, if I don't forgive them, something in my life will go wrong and I can't have that. If I'm angry with them, they'll have power over me and I'd rather live free, then with hate in my heart."

"You can forgive people but you don't have to fuck with them." Ang said and sat on the bed next to me. I had to ask her to get up because my side hurt too bad and any movement, instilled pain.

They all stayed in the room with me for hours. My grandmother asked Tech and Ang, to give her a ride home and promised to come visit me tomorrow. The nurse came in and removed the catheter. I thought he'd be disgusted but he held my hand the entire time. Marco, asked the nurse to assist me in the bathroom to shower. No matter how much pain, I was currently in, I couldn't lay here dirty. When we finished, he was lying asleep on the bed.

"Honey, I don't think he's slept, since they brought you outta surgery." She whispered, so we wouldn't wake him up.

"Really!"

"Yea. I can tell he really loves you too."

"Why is that?" I smiled, staring at him lying there.

"Honey, no one can get in this room without his permission and he even had the floor on lock. Other people visiting, had to do extra sign in's and be checked. Any man that's willing to go the distance for a woman like that, is worth keeping."

"Yea, I think, I'll keep him." She helped me stand and in the bed. I tried my hardest not to wake him but he woke up anyway.

"You want me to get up?"

"No. I need to feel you next to me." The nurse lifted my legs on the bed and put the cover on me.

"Same here ma. I haven't slept good in a very long time." He kissed me and the nurse smiled. She turned the light off and closed the door behind her.

"I love you Marco."

"I love you too. And you're coming home with me, in the morning." I didn't say anything and fell asleep in his arms. If we could stay like this forever, I'd love it.

****

Over the next few days, Marco catered to me, hand and foot. In the morning, he'd bring me down stairs and at night, he'd help me shower and get in the bed. Anything, I wanted, he gave me, with no questions asked. I heard him on the phone a few times with his father, yelling about my aunt. Evidently, she was scared to death and hiding from Marco. I thought it was funny how tough she is, when he wasn't around but scared and nervous, when he was.

****

"WHERE THE FUCK ARE YOU?" He screamed in the phone and I got scared. Why is he yelling and looking for me?

The day Zaire, treated me like shit, I distanced myself away from him. I slid the envelope under his door and do you know, he never even told me about the STD's. I don't know if he thought maybe he didn't give it to me, or the fact he knew, he had it and didn't wanna tell me. Whatever the reason, I knew then, he and I, could never be together or even friends from that point on.

Anyway, we didn't speak for three weeks and when we finally did, he wanted to have sex and I wasn't doing that. He tried to talk to me and I'd tell him, I was super busy. If he came by the dorm, I told them to say, I wasn't there. I had no roommate, so it wasn't hard to keep the room quiet if he did come to the door. I'd put my earphones in the laptop so no one could hear anything. The last day of school, I left early in the morning just to get away and now he's calling me.

"I'm home, Zaire. Why are you screaming?" I stood up and walked to the stairs to see where Marco was. When I didn't see him, I assumed he left.

"I need to see you."

"For what?"

"Because I fucking said so. I'll be there next week and I better see you." He hung the phone up in my ear. I went in the room, got in the bed and cried myself to sleep. I bet, this is my karma for my aunt. Why does bad shit keep happening to me?

Marco

I walked in the hospital room expecting to hear Cara telling Rak, we fucked but seeing Shanta, beating on Rakia, infuriated me. I almost slit her fucking throat, had it not been for my Rak, asking me not to. I wasn't worried about going to jail but the blood on Rakia's face and how bad she was crying, did something to me. I had murder on my mind and the person, I wanted to die, is Shanta.

My father, had been calling me damn near every day, asking me not to kill her. All of a sudden, she fears for her life, yet, gave no fucks, when she beat on Rak. She probably didn't expect me to walk in and she knew her niece wouldn't tell on her. As luck would have it, I saw it all and couldn't wait to get my hands on her. I'm gonna let her breathe right now and believe, I'm over it. But no one's gonna be able to stop me, once I get her.

****

I came home from being out all day and noticed, somebody was cooking in the kitchen. I was so used to never being here, it wasn't expected. I walked down the hall to see Rakia, holding Antoine Jr. and checking the food. Ang, was reading a magazine at the table. I walked over, mushed her in the head and took my godson, from Rak. She sucked her teeth and I ignored her. She may be his godmother but the men, had to stick together.

"You hungry babe?" She asked and kissed my lips.

"Depends. What's on the menu?"

"Ugh, other people are in the house." Ang, raised her hand.

"I got you later baby." She whispered and my dick twitched. I hadn't had sex with anyone, since she's been here. Bobbi, blew my phone up but the only woman in my life, is Rak and no one is changing that.

"Did you have a good day?" Me and Ang, both looked at her.

"WHAT!" She whined.

"Am I not supposed to ask?" The front door opened and Tech came strolling in with an evil look on his face. Ang, took lil man and I walked in my home office. He shut the door and sat down.

"Dude, is here."

"What you mean, he's here?"

"You heard me."

"What the fuck is he doing here?"

"I don't know but we're watching his boys. We haven't been able to locate him, yet." I stared out my window. This is what I did, when I had something on my mind and needed to find an answer.

"Tell the guys to keep an eye on his crew because he's bound to meet up with them. In the meantime, everyone needs to have their eyes open. He could be trying to befriend people, in hopes, to get at us."

"You got it. What's up with you and Rak?"

"Man, I don't even know. She's so guarded, and its hard to get her to come out of her shell. I tried to give her

253

privacy but she won't go to sleep, until I'm lying next to her."
He started laughing.

"I'm serious. Remember the other night, when we were handling business." I spoke about the guy we had to murk because we found out he was the mole and giving this Z guy, information. Lucky, we had enough time to change our drop off and pick up's, before he could hit. I'm sure, it's the reason, he came here.

"I got home at four and she was sitting up, waiting for me. I could tell, she was tired because her eyes were red as hell. Bro, when I laid down and put the covers over my legs, she laid on my chest and I swear, thirty seconds later she was knocked out."

"Well, be good to her this time bro. She's a good one and good for you."

"I know and I'ma do right." We walked out and Rakia had a smile on her face.

"What?"

"Ummm, your mom, is here." I looked past her and sure enough, my mom was on the couch. Tech, ran over and gave her a hug. I, on the other hand, took my time.

"What?"

"Marco. Don't talk to your mom like that." Rakia smacked me on the arm and my mother smirked.

"I like her, for you." I sucked my teeth.

"You don't even know her."

"Whose fault is that?"

"Yours." She laughed.

"Marco, I came by because your lowlife father, wants me to ask you, not to kill his ugly ass girlfriend."

"He should be worried about more important things, then a woman attacking a chick, she knew couldn't fight. Then, she had the nerve to talk shit afterwards but hiding behind pops."

"Same thing, I said." She shrugged her shoulders.

See, my mom, hated my dad for cheating on her years ago. It wasn't with Shanta but she came shortly after and my mom left him. She took half of everything he had and still gets alimony, once a month. He always says, she was the one who got away but he didn't change his ways. Shit, I don't even know why he going so hard for Shanta, when he has a couple other chicks, he fucks. My mom moved on and is dating some attorney. They're always traveling, which is why I told her, she should blame herself for not meeting Rak.

"Dinner is ready." Rak said and I had to control myself when she removed the apron. I knew she was dressed under it but the shirt she had on, showed her stomach and the belly ring, she must've gotten away at school. Then her pussy print was extra fat in the leggings.

"Come here Rak." Tech, walked past shaking his head.

"What?" She wrapped her arms around my neck and I lifted her up. *Fuck dinner*. I'm about to make love to her.

"Marco, you have company."

"We have company. This is your house too, so stop excluding yourself." I locked the door and walked over to her.

"We have company and.-"

"And nothing. They know, what's up." I stood her up and pulled the leggings down.

"You did this on purpose." She smirked and stepped outta them. Rak, didn't have any panties on and her pussy was freshly shaved. The first time we had sex, she had hair down there and it never bothered me. I guess, she wanted to try something new.

"I did this too." She took her shirt off and pointed to a small tattoo on her chest. There was a M and a R, in a heart. I looked at her and if I didn't know before, I knew now. She is the person, I've been waiting for, to settle down with. I placed a kiss on it and she winced out in pain.

"My bad." I wiped my lips off because she had some of that ointment on it.

"Did you miss me?" I lifted her on my shoulders and she held on tight. My tongue flickered around her clit.

"Yessssssss. God, I love you so much." She moaned and her juices seeped out and in my mouth. I let her get a few more off, before putting her down and pulling my man out.

"Marco, I'm scared to catch a disease." She said and asked me to wear a condom. I lifted her face and she was crying.

"What's wrong?" She didn't respond.

"I would never risk your health, by giving you a disease." I pulled my clothes up.

"You don't wanna have sex now?"

"Ma, I don't have any condoms and if you want me to wear protection, we have to wait until later."

"But, I'm horny."

"Shit, me too but I'll always respect your choice." She nodded and stood in front of me.

"You gotta move Rak, or put some clothes on." She sat on my lap and slid her tongue in my mouth.

"Shit." She was grinding her bottom half on my lap. Each second, it was getting harder for me not to say, fuck it. I guess she did because she pulled my man out and slid down. I let my hands roam up and down her back, as we continued kissing.

"You feel so fucking good, Rak." I guided her in circles and felt myself getting ready to cum. I didn't even care, if it was early. She had some banging ass pussy. I let go and so did she. I flipped her over and lifted her legs on my shoulder, while

I slid my man up and down her slits. My dick grew fast as hell and I almost drowned this time, when I dove in. I was hitting shit, she ain't never felt before and we both knew it, from the way she moaned and scratched my back.

"I love you Marco. Please don't hurt me again."

"I won't. Give it to me." I felt her treasure swelling up and soon after, she burst all over me. I put her on all fours and the sight of her ass jiggling, had a nigga gone.

"Yes, baby. Yesssss." She screamed out. Rakia, came so many times, that when we finally finished after the third time, I had to wash her up in the bed. I looked at the clock and it was after eleven and my ass was starving.

I went downstairs and everyone was gone. The kitchen was cleaned and there were two plates on the counter, wrapped in aluminum foil. Ang, left us a note saying, we should've fucked when they left. I tossed it in the trash and laughed. I heated both our plates up and took two water bottles out the fridge. I shut the lights off downstairs, made sure the door was locked and the alarm was on. I couldn't wait to fuck this food up. There was fried chicken, fresh string beans, corn on the cob and some yellow rice. I don't care how many starches was on my plate, a nigga was about to dog this.

"Get up Rak." I sat the plate down next to her and put mine on the other side. I got in bed and kissed the back of her neck.

"I don't wanna Marco." She was cute, when she whined.

"I know but we gotta eat. I promise, to leave you alone, afterwards." She groaned a little and sat up.

"Baby, I could've ate tomorrow."

"Nah, you need to eat with your man."

"I guess so." She picked her plate up and ended up eating the rice, off mine and I ate the corn, off hers.

"Can I go to bed now?" I leaned over and gave her a kiss.

"You can now."

"Thank you. I need to be ready for you in the morning. I know this ain't over." She pulled the covers up to her neck and rolled over. I smacked her on the ass, under the covers.

"Long as you know."

****

"Fuck." I moaned out as Rak, started riding the shit outta me. For someone who was a virgin, I'm glad she learned quick.

"Make me cum, papi." I stopped all movement and looked at her.

"Say that shit again." She grinded a little.

"Mmmmm, make me cum, papiiiiii." This time she said it with a little extra added, and I swear, my dick got harder. The way she said it and the way her body moved at the same time, had me in a zone. I sat up, pulled her face to mine and aggressively kissed and fucked her from the bottom.

"Am I good enough for you?"

"Hell yea, Rak." I made her cum like she asked and in return, she flipped on all fours, threw her ass back and had me doing the same. I laid on the side of her, after we finished and stared.

"Shorty, you're it for me. I don't want anyone else."

"Really!" I could hear the excitement in her voice.

"Really. Now, come take a shower with me. I got some things to do today."

"Ok." She followed me in the bathroom and of course, we had sex in there. We both got dressed, and I left her at the house, with money and a sore ass pussy. She loved the truck and told me, she was taking it for a ride today. I told her to be careful and made sure one of the guards, kept an eye on her. I couldn't take the chance of her stupid ass aunt, Bobbi, Cara or anyone else bothering her, for that matter. I'm murking all of them eventually and make it look like an accident. If Rak, finds out the truth, she'll just have to be mad but their time is coming.

Rakia

"This is nice, Rak." Ang said when I picked her up from the house. She said, Tech left out this morning, to meet up with Marco and she didn't want to stay home.

"I know right. I had no idea, he even got it for me."

"Girl, that man loves you." I started smiling.

"And I love him too, Ang. I'm scared, he's gonna hurt me."

"Look, Rak. He messed up and you took him back. If you plan on being with him, let the shit he did, go."

"I have."

"I'm not making an excuse but the two times he slept with others, you did tell him, to leave and never come back." I glanced over at her and back at the road.

"He shouldn't have automatically run to another woman but you gave him the ok, to do it." I nodded my head. I understood what she said and I learned, if I don't want him to do something, don't give him the idea, he can.

The two of us drove to Shore Hills mall, and shopped until we dropped. I mean, we went in so many stores, I never even dreamed about and purchased things, I would've never been able to afford, had it not been for him. To show my appreciation, I did stop in some female stores and get a few outfits, I'm sure he'd like to see on me. Ang, told me to get some heels too, because men love fucking a woman in them, for some reason. Then she proceeded to tell me some of the freaky things her and Tech, do. I thought Marco did some things but boy, they were on some X-rated shit. I couldn't wait to get on that level.

We stopped in Ruby Tuesday's to eat and luckily, it wasn't that crowded. We both ate from the salad bar and waited for the entrée to come out. As we sat there, I looked over the new phone I got. It was the IPhone 8 plus and I fell in love with the rose gold one. It was crazy putting it in my name. I guess because the state phone was in my grandma's and nothing else, had my name on it. I asked the man to activate it, in the store so I could use it. I called Marco's phone and he didn't answer. I called back a few times and after the 5th time, he finally picked up.

"WHO THE FUCK IS THIS?" He shouted and Ang, heard him too.

"Ummmm. Its Rakia. I'm gonna call you back."

"No ma. I'm sorry. I didn't mean to yell at you. Whose number is this?" I felt at ease, once he said that.

"I got a new phone at the mall and I wanted to make sure you had the number. If you're busy, you can call me back. I don't wanna bother you."

"Relax ma. I'm not upset. I don't usually answer calls from people, I don't know. Why didn't you text me?"

"I don't know. I wanted to hear your voice." Ang, was shaking her head and grinning.

"Mmmm hmmm. You want some of papi's dick, huh?"

"Maybe." I bit down on my lip and tried to stop blushing.

"I got you later. Did you enjoy yourself at the mall?"

"I'm ready Marco." I heard some woman say. I became upset.

"Don't you see me on the phone with my future wife? Back the fuck up, yo."

"I'll see you later."

"Rak, it's not what you think, so don't wreck your brain tryna figure it out. If you wanna know, just ask."

"I didn't say anything."

"But I know you. You may not say anything but you're thinking it. I'm at the warehouse and she's one of the accountants. One thing, I won't do, is lie to you Rak. If you ever wanna stop by, feel free. I told you, you're my woman and I'm not gonna mess up. I love you too much for that."

"Damn. Whatever you said Marco, has her smiling real hard." Ang, yelled and he started laughing.

"I'll see you, when I get home. I love you Rak."

"I love you too." I ended the call and looked up to see Ang, smirking.

"I'm happy for you Rakia. You deserve every bit of happiness, he's about to give you." I nodded my head and dug into the steak, I ordered. It felt good to finally have someone love me, the way, I love them. After we ate, we walked out, with all our bags.

****

"Why does the other phone keep ringing?" Ang, asked. I hadn't disconnected the state phone yet.

"Zaire, is in town and wants to see me." She stopped walking and looked at me.

"Not a good idea Rak."

"I don't know what to do. He keeps calling and threatening me, if I don't."

"Tell Marco."

"I can't."

"WHAT?"

"He may think, I want him and that's far from the truth." My phone rang again and this time; it was my grandmother. She wanted me to stop by and Ang, wouldn't let me go without her.

Once we pulled up, my cousin Rahmel, came to the truck and I told him no, right off the back. This car was not given to me and I didn't want Marco, getting upset. Yes, its mine but he purchased it, so my cousin won't be driving in it. He did say how nice it was and how he wanted to go for a ride with me. I told him after, I spoke to my grandmother he could come with me, to drop Ang off.

I walked in the house, and my aunt, Cara and my grandmother were at the table. I turned around to leave. Ang, asked me what was wrong because she hadn't walked in yet. Tech, called her right before we got out the car. I could hear my grandmother calling me and I didn't wanna be rude but there's no way, my aunt or anyone else, will put hands on me. I called Marco, and he answered right away. He could tell how upset I was and said, he was on the way and to go back to my truck. I hate, getting him involved but I don't wanna fight or end up in the hospital again.

"Oh, you too cute, to be around your family? This nigga, brought you a new truck and you the shit now." Cara said, coming out the door.

"I don't wanna argue with you. Grandma, is this what you called me for?" She came off the porch and towards me. She put her hands on my face and stared in my eyes.

"I wanted the three of you to make up. Rakia, I would never have you come here, if I knew this would happen. They claimed to want to make things right. I should've known better. Baby, I'm sorry. Get in your truck and leave." I nodded and started walking over to it.

"Take your ho ass, the fuck up outta here." I stopped and turned around. I shouldn't be saying anything but with Marco coming, I felt a little bold. I made my way over to Cara.

"Oh shit." I heard Rahmel say. He hated Cara, which is the reason, he barely ever came around them. He moved out of the house at seventeen and never went back and I can't say, I blame him.

"I've had enough of your shit." Everyone looked shocked.

"I have always been there for you Cara. I forgave you, for all the mean and cruel things you did and said to me but it doesn't matter because your evil." She laughed and so did my aunt.

"Evil, ain't the word for how, I'm going to be moving forward. You stole my man, like the slut you are and out here, portraying yourself to be, holier than thou."

"Stole your man, who? We all know Marco, has never claimed a woman before me and he won't afterwards. Why are you so obsessed over him anyway?" Just as I asked, there was a loud noise. I looked and my aunt, had taken a baseball bat and started bashing the windows out of my truck.

"OH MY GOD!" My grandmother yelled out. I stood there with tears coming down my face because they hated me so much, this is what it came to.

"Fuck this." Ang walked over to Cara and started whooping her ass, while Rahmel, ran over to his mom and snatched the bat from her. It didn't matter because she had already gotten every window busted, except for the front windshield. After he took the bat, I notice her walk to the tires and the hissing sound, was very loud.

"Yo, ma, what the fuck you doing? Why you tearing her shit up?" Rahmel snatched her up and tossed her on the ground. He was fuming now and all I could do was sit on the curb and rock back and forth. How could my day, get any worse?

"Get your ass up, and follow me." I looked on the side of me and was snatched up by the arm. I noticed a big guy coming in my direction.

POW! POW! He shot him. I froze because not only have I never seen a man get shot, but why was he carrying a gun?

"RAKIA!" I heard Ang shouting and tried to go back to her. He threw me in the truck and told me if I ran, he'd kill me, like he did the guy. I sat there staring out the window at all the chaos going on. *How did my life get this bad?*

Angela

"I'm sick of you, bitch." I kicked Cara once more in the face and went looking for Rakia. I know this was a lot for her. I admit, when she told me her grandmother called and invited her over, I was very skeptical, as I should be. Not of her grandma but for this shit going down right here.

Her aunt came out, swinging a bat at her truck, for no damn reason. Cara, popping shit about Marco being hers from the start, when we all know, Rakia, peeped him first. I remember the day, like it was yesterday because it was the first time, I saw my husband, Tech.

"Lil mama. Come here for a minute." The guy called me from his Porsche truck. Usually, I don't entertain grown men. I'm ok, dealing with my young high school guys. They're harmless and you can pretty much, play a lotta mind games with them. Cara, was so engrossed in showing her assets off, for the local hustla's, she paid me no mind and I'm happy.

Unfortunately, I knew exactly, the type of chick she was and didn't want her trying to get at this guy.

"What's up?" I had my books in my arm.

"How old are you?"

"I just turned eighteen last week. Why?"

"I had to make sure, you were legal before I asked for your number." I put my head down, blushing.

"You gonna give it to me, or what?" I must've had my head down too long.

"Ummm sure." Just as I was about to say it, a black truck pulled up with tinted windows and everyone started acting crazy. The guys had stopped shooting dice and stood at attention. It's obvious, whoever was in the car, is the boss. I saw him step out and noticed Rakia, standing there, staring like a star struck teenager. It was funny because she never looked at boys or men, for that matter. I turned around to give him my number and his phone rang.

"Yea, I been here for a minute. Nah, they good. I'm on the way." He hung up and instead of asking for my number again, he pulled off. I was pissed because he was sexy and

273

grown. I made my way to Cara, who had just walked to Rakia

and started fucking with her, as usual.

I hated the way, Cara acted towards her but being her

friend, I entertained the shit. I did feel bad when Cara, told her

she was special and the guy, was hers. Shanta, always instilled

in them, never to sleep with the same guy because it would

cause major problems. We had no idea what she was talking

about at the time.

Anyway, I take full responsibility for treating her

fucked up, which is why, the night of graduation, I stayed at the

club, even after Cara left. I refused to continue harassing and

hurting her. I was also scared, something bad would happen

and knowing Rakia, she wouldn't know what to do. The

jealousy and hatred Cara held for her cousin, is beyond

pathetic. When she wished rape on us, I wanted to beat her ass

but would've gotten thrown out the club and Rakia would've

been alone.

After she went in VIP with Marco, someone sat next to

me. Before, I looked, he spoke and I could barely hear him. I

turned around and it was the same guy from the truck, a year

274

earlier, at the bodega. He looked so damn good up close. Before Rakia came back, he and I exchanged phone numbers and from that moment on, we've been together, minus the setback with the stripper bitch.

Anyway, Cara has wanted Marco, for almost two years now and he wants no parts of her; however, she does the most to get him. I never understood, how a woman can run behind a man, who doesn't want them. Just move the fuck on.

I turned around, to see some guy dragging Rak, to a car. I yelled her name and could tell she tried to get away but lost my voice, when he shot some guy. It was like everyone froze, when the gunshots rang out. Who the fuck is this guy and why does he have her? Is he an enemy of Marco, or is it the guy, who she's been seeing at the school and threatening her? Right now, I couldn't think straight as he peeled off the street. I was stuck because her truck was fucked up, so I couldn't follow them.

"Baby, where are you?" I asked Tech, the minute he answered his phone.

"Two minutes away. What's wrong? You good? Is Rakia, ok?"

"Everything's wrong. Baby, hurry up and get here, someone took Rakia." The line went dead and I could see, cops coming down the street. Who the hell called them? We in the hood, and no one calls 5 0.

"I'm gonna make sure you go to jail." Cara said behind me and I noticed her mom, running to some car.

"You called the cops. Bitch, you know it's no snitching in the fucking hood."

"That may be what you live by but when I want something or someone, I make sure, everyone blocking, is outta my way."

"What the fuck are you talking about?"

"Well, it seems like Marco, won't have anything to do with me; therefore, Tech, is the next best thing." I swung so hard, she tumbled back but didn't fall.

"Officer, did you see her attack me?" I turned around and sure enough, two officers were coming towards us.

"Yes, we did. Ma'am, put your hands behind your back." I did like he asked.

"Don't worry bitch. I'll make sure Tech is well taken care of, like before." She shouted and as bad as, I wanted to ask what she meant, I couldn't.

"Wait!" I heard her coming closer.

"Don't you wanna know, what I mean?" She was taunting the shit outta me. She had a bloody nose from me beating her up and she was still popping shit.

"YO, GET THOSE FUCKING CUFFS OFF HER." I heard Tech yell and smiled at Cara. She rolled her eyes.

"What happened, Ang?"

"Sir, we can't. She attacked this woman and.-" It was like he didn't hear anything else and wrapped his hands around her throat. The cops were trying hard as hell to get his hands off.

"Bro, come on. You know. She won't be at the station long." Tech let go and backed away.

"I'll be behind the cop car." He kissed me and backed up.

"Fuck you and her, Tech." The cop put me in the car and before he closed the door, Cara had a smirk on her face, as she wiped the blood off her lip.

"Ang, did Tech tell you about the time we fucked?" I put my foot out so the cop couldn't close the door.

"What did you say?"

"Nothing, Ang. I'll be down there."

"No, Tech. You don't get to make me look crazy. Both of you niggas, try and hide the shit you did with me and for what? To save face. Fuck that. Ang, I sucked and fucked your man. Oh, excuse me; your husband." I looked at him.

"Shut the fuck up."

"Why you think, he was so mad at the block party, when I asked if you were ready to leave and when I came to get my stuff from your house, before you went to school? He didn't wanna tell you and has been paying me, to keep my mouth shut." Marco and I, both stared at him.

"Yea, all the new shit I'm rocking, is courtesy of your husband. Damn, it feels good to get that shit off my chest.

Officers, I'll be down to make a statement." She said and I moved my leg so he could close the door.

"Ang."

"Can you pull off, officer?" I turned my head and let the tears fall. I didn't want him or her, to see how bad the shit she said, hurt me. She was my friend and he was my man. How could he do this to me?

"ANG." He banged on the window and I still refused to look at him.

"Ma'am, we're gonna let you go." The officer said, when we left.

"Huh?"

"We work for them and as you know, they won't allow us to bring you there."

"Can you take me to my parents' house, please?" I gave him the address and sat in the back of the car, letting the tears fall down my face. All of a sudden, there were gunshots going off and the car was getting hit. I laid on the seat but nothing could prepare me for the pain, I was experiencing. My body was on fire and my eyes, were closing. *God, please don't let me die.*

Marco

"Rahmel, what the fuck happened out here and where's my girl?" He was standing next to me as the EMT's, put one of my guards on a stretcher.

"Man, my mom, attacked Rakia's car; Ang, beat my sister up and some dude, came outta nowhere, walked up on Rak, and made her get in the car with him."

"What the fuck, you just say?" I had him yoked up against the car.

"Marco, I know you love my cousin and trust me, if I could've saved her, I would've. I was so busy trying to get my mom and stop the fight, that none of us paid attention, to Rakia. We heard gunshots and the dude was on the ground. By the time, we looked, some guy had her in the car, pulling off." I let him go.

"FUCK! Was she hit? Who is the dude?"

"I don't know. I've never seen him before, and you know, I know everyone." I nodded because he really did.

Rahmel, isn't a street nigga but he was cool, with all the hood dudes. On a few occasions, I let him parlay in VIP with us, when we went out just because he was Rakia's cousin and the only one, besides his grandmother, who looked out for her.

"What kind of car was it?"

"It was black, with tinted windows and dark enough, where I couldn't see in." I looked at Tech, who was stressing the fuck out over the shit, Cara told Ang. I had to make him stay with me and not get Ang from the station, right away. I told him, she needed time to figure shit out and he could explain it later. When a woman is that angry, its best to give her space.

"Where's your mother?"

"Man, I don't know. The bitch went running to some car and left." I nodded.

"Marco." I turned around and saw Rak's grandmother coming in my direction.

"I'm so sorry. I didn't mean for this to happen."

"What exactly happened?" She explained, how she called Rak over because she wanted the three of them to make

282

up. She was over the fighting and pettiness, between them. I understood why but I also told her, it wasn't a good idea, without having me there to protect her. Not that, I'm a savior but I damn sure am, Rakia's. She agreed and begged me to find her.

"I am. Go in the house and I'll call you, when I have her." I kissed her cheek. Tech and I, headed over to my truck and got inside.

"Who you think, could have her?"

"Man, I have no idea. Rakia, doesn't have any enemies and forgave everybody, no matter how fucked up they were to her. She had to know this person or even feel like, he wasn't a threat. At least, it's what I'm thinking but the questions is, who?

We drove to the police station to get Ang and it looked like the shit was deserted. He opened the door and we walked to the captain's office. He wasn't there, which is weird because Tech called and mentioned Ang, would be coming and he said, he'd be there. The only person here right now was the old ass lady, doing dispatch. She had to be related to someone, in order to have this position. We both approached her at the desk and she rolled her eyes, as if we did something to her.

"If you want something, open your mouth." Tech and I, both started laughing. How her old ass in here talking shit?

"Yo, where the captain at?" She turned around and looked behind her and then under the desk.

"Well, he ain't in here, now is he?"

"Bitch, I'll fuck you up in here." Tech had her by the shirt.

"Yo, let her old ass go." She had a petrified look on her face.

"Bet yo ass, ain't tough now."

"I could have you arrested?" She was shaking.

"By who? Ain't a motherfucker, in this place. What the hell is going on and where is the captain?"

"Since, you asked nicely, I guess, I could tell you." I had about enough of her ass.

"Someone shot up a police car and all available units are in route there."

"Oh word? Somebody bold as hell for that?" Just as this shit was happening a text message came to my phone. I opened it and wasn't prepared for the shit, I saw.

"I'm gonna kill Rakia." I was ready to go. I told him to get the information needed so we could get Ang, because murder was all over my brain.

"Where's the woman, who's supposed to be dropped off?" Tech asked and she gave him a sympathetic stare. I looked at him and his demeanor was unreadable.

"What?"

"The cop car that was shot up, had a woman passenger in the back. I'm sorry." It was like all the blood drained from his face and he fell against the wall. I asked for the address where the shooting was. I would deal with Rakia later because his news, is worse. We drove to the scene and shit was taped off. Caution tape, cops and detectives were everywhere and the coroners truck was there.

"You ok?" I asked and turned to look at him. I saw a few tears coming down his face.

"Bro, I can't get out."

285

"Tech, you have to." He sat there for a few minutes and finally opened the door.

When we made our way through the crowd, the scene was much worse, than I could imagine. Tech, stood there frozen and out the corner of my eye, I noticed someone, who in my opinion could only be there, if they were responsible. Tech, must've seen the same person, because he took off running and outta nowhere, shots rang out.

"TECHHHHHHHHHH!"

TO BE CONTINUED...